# EERIE TALES OF TERROR AND DREAD

Bernhardt J. Hurwood

SCHOLASTIC INC.
New York Toronto London Auckland Sydney

If you purchased this book without a cover, you should be aware that this book is stolen property. It was reported as "unsold and destroyed" to the publisher, and neither the author nor the publisher has received any payment for this "stripped book."

No part of this publication may be reproduced in whole or in part, or stored in a retrieval system, or transmitted in any form or by any means, electronic, mechanical, photocopying, recording, or otherwise, without written permission of the publisher. For information regarding permission, write to Scholastic Inc., 730 Broadway, New York, NY 10003.

ISBN 0-590-44650-9

Copyright © 1973 by Bernhardt J. Hurwood.
All rights reserved. Published by Scholastic Inc.
POINT is a registered trademark of Scholastic Inc.

12 11 10 9 8 7 6 5 4 3 2          2 3 4 5 6/9

# CONTENTS

# THE MAGICIAN

GLISTENING RIVULETS of sweat dripped down The Great Cosmo's forehead as he went through the genuinely exhausting motions of pushing the wicked looking saw back and forth. Sniggers and titters of laughter went through the audience, and he thought to himself, "It's no use, I'm not getting through to them." He had good reason to be concerned. The hooting and periodic outbursts of the audience had made him so nervous that almost every trick he tried to perform somehow went wrong. Several times he had wanted to drop everything and run offstage, but sheer will power forced him to continue in spite of everything.

He had wanted to be a magician all his life. As a boy he had dreamed endlessly of a glittering career as "The Great Cosmo." It had been the driving force behind everything he did, but somehow he grew older, the years went by, and the dream kept evading him.

Oh, sure enough, he came to be known as "The Great Cosmo." He became a professional magician, but with the competition of movies, television, and rock musicians, he never managed to progress beyond the arenas of second rate circuses, shoddy nightclubs, and cheap carnivals.

Now, performing for the first time in his life as a featured act in a real theater, he found himself unable to seize the imagination of the audience. He kept losing control and they laughed and giggled when they should have been oohing and ahhing. They were too aware, too sure of themselves, and the old sawing-the-woman-in-half trick simply didn't impress them.

"Don't worry, darling," whispered his wife from inside one half of the trick box. "We'll go out to some nice place afterwards and celebrate our opening here."

A musical fanfare prevented his answering as the two halves of the box "broke" in two. The Great Cosmo forced a smile as he bowed low and waited for the applause that never came.

"And now, my dear friends," he announced, hoping against hope that his voice wouldn't crack, "I will present to you the most mystifying feat of my repertoire, known only to myself and select masters of the Orient. . . ."

"Big deal!" came a derisive cackle.

"Let's see you turn into a motel!" jeered another raucous voice.

There was more laughter, but The Great Cosmo went on. "Before your very eyes, using neither mechanical aid nor electronic contrivance, I shall cause the lovely lady to disappear."

That was the cue for his wife to walk out

on stage, smile, and take a bow. She was a very pretty woman, and her presence inspired applause and whistles of appreciation in place of the catcalls and jeers that had filled the air only moments before.

"Please, please, don't let anything go wrong," prayed the magician silently to himself as he led his wife to the stool that had been placed at dead center of the cleared stage. She seated herself, confident that she could hold the audience with her smile, crossing her legs and resting her hands on the edge of the stool. Then her husband whipped a billowing piece of colored fabric from a concealed hollow tube behind them. It was "the mystical cloak of invisibility" that would cause her to vanish from sight. The audience fell grudgingly silent as an ominous drum flourish began rising from the orchestra pit and The Great Cosmo flung the cloak over his smiling assistant.

"And now," he intoned solemnly, "I shall utter the mysterious incantation taken directly from the ancient Egyptian Book of the Dead. . . ." He paused for effect and muttered a few words of impressive gibberish, facing the audience, his arms outflung and his head thrown back.

Suddenly a gasp — a collective intake of breath arose from the audience as though from a single throat. The Great Cosmo felt a chill. What were they doing? He had barely begun to perform the illusion. Before he had a chance even to collect his thoughts the applause began. It began with only a trickle of clapping, and then the sound rose to a thunderous crescendo of cheering, roaring, stomping, mingled with cries of "Bravo! Bravo!"

Confused, startled, hardly daring to believe what was happening he took a few steps backward, bowed low, and indicated the stool with his right hand. Only seconds before it had supported his wife and now stood empty, save for the colored cloak that was draped loosely over it. He had enough presence of mind to snatch the cloak up and run off stage while the cheering still was at its height. He assumed that Doreen had done something unexpected to surprise him.

"Go on, go back and take a bow," said the stage manager.

"I'll wait for Doreen," replied The Grea Cosmo.

"Where the devil is she?" demanded the chief stagehand. "What did you do to her? There wasn't even a trap door!"

"Never mind the questions now!" ordered the stage manager. "The audience is going crazy. Go on out, take some bows."

"But...but..." began the magician, a chilling sensation creeping up his back.

"Get out there, man!" interrupted the stage manager, grabbing him by the shoulder and pushing him toward the stage and the cheering audience.

"More! More!" the audience shouted as they applauded and stomped, whistled and yelled. His heart pounded with excitement, but it was not of the sort he had yearned for all his life. What should have been the most

8

triumphant moment of his career was now tainted by something unknown and alarming. He knew that if he didn't get off stage immediately he was going to be sick. So, with his lips still stretched apart in a mirthless grin, he bowed again, then turned and hurried into the wings as quickly as he could, stopping neither for the words of congratulation nor the questions that now seemed to bombard his ears from all directions.

Doreen had played a little trick on him, that was all. She was probably up in the dressing room waiting. She had always had a wonderful sense of humor, and she had done this to surprise and please him. Breathing heavily, he seized the narrow iron railing of the circular backstage staircase and began running up its tight spiral two steps at a time. The clatter of his feet drowned out all other sounds. The dressing room was at the end of the corridor, and when he got to the top of the stairs he ran all the way.

Grabbing the doorknob he rushed into the room without knocking. "Doreen!" he began, but the rest of the sentence was choked off before he could get it out. The dressing room was empty.

There was his wife's purse before the mirror on her dressing table, just as she had left it before going down to do the act. He remembered how he had chided her on leaving it like that, but she had laughed and said, "What's there to steal from me?" Her street clothes were neatly arranged exactly as she had left them.

9

A terrible feeling of panic overcame The Great Cosmo. It made no sense. She had to be somewhere in the theater. She had to be! I know, he thought, she's playing a practical joke on me. She's hiding somewhere. . . .

Running from the room he began knocking on doors, calling, "Doreen, Doreen, are you there?" Silence greeted him.

He should have known better, of course. Even though he had never performed as a featured attraction in one, he was no stranger to backstages of theaters. But he was upset and wasn't thinking straight. Climbing up to the flies, directly above the stage where scenic backdrops were suspended, he caught his foot, plunged forward, and hit his head. Everything went black.

When he regained his senses Cosmo had no idea of how much time had passed. All he knew was that there was a terrible throbbing pain in his head and a dry bad taste in his mouth. It took him a few moments to remember where he was, and as everything came tumbling back to his mind the terrible feeling of panic and dread returned. Trembling all over he crawled on his hands and knees to the narrow catwalk that would take him back to the ladder leading down to the dressing room floor. He knew that several hours must have passed because the theater was completely dark.

He had to grope his way to the dressing room, and when he got there he had no feeling of relief. The lights would not go on. Then he remembered that after the performances, after all the people had left the theater, the night watchman threw the main switch and cut off the electricity. That was no problem for The Great Cosmo. He had played too many out-of-the-way places. He always carried a supply of candles; besides, there were always one or two candle tricks. . . .

Breathing heavily he rummaged through his prop trunk until he found a candle. His first attempt at lighting it was a dismal failure, his hand trembled so. But finally the room was bathed in its soft flickering glow.

"Doreen!" he called out, raising the candle and looking about the room. There was no answer. Everything was as before. The purse, the clothes, even the half-eaten sandwich left over from lunch. Maybe she went back to the hotel, he thought. But he didn't really believe that. He knew her too well. She wouldn't just leave like that. Besides, she never would go out on the street wearing nothing but a stage costume.

Was it possible that . . . "Don't be crazy, Cosmo!" he snarled aloud. "You're an illusionist, a trickster . . . there's no such thing as real magic!"

Now he was seated before his own dressing table, looking in the mirror, and talking to himself. There was a bad gash on his head where he had bumped it and the jagged mark left by the dried blood looked even worse in the dim flickering candlelight. "It was only a simple trick," he said to his reflection, pleadingly. "I didn't even finish it. All I did was say. . . ." The string of nonsense syllables that

11

he had uttered earlier on stage came back with vivid clarity, flashing before his eyes as though on a glowing neon sign. Had he read them somewhere? Had he made them up? Maybe it was a combination of both. A strange expression came over his face as he looked in the mirror and formed the exact words again. Was that a large dark shape looming up behind him that cast a weirdly solid shadow in the mirror? Or was the combination of candlelight and darkness playing tricks on him? He whirled around and held the candle up. Nothing. His heart now pounded in his chest like a trip-hammer. He turned again and looked in the mirror. Now it was more than a shadow. It was something unspeakably horrible taking shape.... He spun around again, drawing in his breath in terror. The room was empty, but it had grown cold as a freezer. Then the candle went out ... blackness ... silence ... nothing.

"It jes' don't make sense, Mr. Aikens," said the night watchman before he left in the morning. "I thought I sorta heerd somethin' up by the dressin' rooms. Well, I went up there, an' sure enough, that Mr. Cosmo's door was open. There wuz a funny smell. Like somethin' wuz burnin', y'know what I mean. Wasn't nothin' there, wasn't nobody around, neither. I dunno how the mirror got broke though. Wasn't that kinda sound I heerd. What I can't figger though, is how Mr. Cosmo left. He sure ain't around anymore."

# THE MYSTERIOUS SERPENT

MANY YEARS AGO a young man named Chang lived in a small village that nestled on the shores of the South China Sea. He worked very hard at often distasteful jobs in order to earn enough money to pursue his studies, which he hoped one day would enable him to enter the service of the emperor as a magistrate. Chang's chief amusement was to go sailing in a small junk that he had built himself, and in which he would ply the coastal waters during whatever free hours he had. In time he became a very proficient sailor.

One day there came to Chang's ears word of a small island with no name, a beautiful dot of green snuggled in the blue of the sea. It was a fabled place where flowers were said to bloom the year around, and where the forest was so thick with tangled vines and tall trees, that no man could cross from one side to the other without a hatchet or a sword. Furthermore (Chang had heard), the island had never been inhabited and was believed to be a dwelling place of demons and evil spirits.

Being a brave young man as well as a curious one, Chang decided one summer when he had several free days to sail to the island and explore it in person. Although he tried to convince himself that this was not his real reason for going there, he entertained a secret hope that it might be a hiding place of buried treasure.

The island's whereabouts was no secret, and so after laying in sufficient food and water to last him for the duration of his short voyage, Chang set forth. It was a beautiful summer morning. The sea was calm, yet a steady gentle breeze wafted over the water with sufficent strength to fill the sails of the little junk.

By noon Chang caught sight of his destination on the horizon, and as he neared the shore a delicious scent of flowers caressed his face and he breathed deeply of its perfume. Soon he came close enough to see the land, and trimming his sails he circled the island until he found a suitable spot to disembark.

Before going ashore, he prepared himself a meal which he ate hurriedly since he was anxious to explore the beautiful island. After securing the boat he proceeded to the beach and began walking toward the thick foliage of creepers and ferns amidst the trees. Pausing for a moment, Chang wondered if he had better not go back to the boat and get a hatchet, for the forest looked impenetrable. Suddenly he heard the unmistakable sound of a young woman's laughter directly behind him. Spinning around he was astonished to see a beautiful girl standing in a clump of wild roses. She had long black hair, and a face like porcelain, and she was clad in a long blue silk gown embroidered with flowers and birds. Her eyes sparkled like black diamonds and her lips were ruby red. "I am most happy to see you here," she said in a voice like the tinkling of silver bells. "I did not think I should ever be fortunate enough to meet you."

"Who are you?" asked Chang in amazement.

She lowered her eyes and replied, "I am only a poor singing girl who was carried away from her home and taken here by The Lord of the Sea."

Upon hearing this Chang's heart sank. The Lord of the Sea was an infamous pirate captain whose very name struck terror into those who heard it. There was not a single village along the coast that he had not plundered at one time or another, and he was known to be cruel and merciless to everyone who aroused his anger.

"There is no need to fear," said the girl, "for my master is away on a voyage and will not return for many weeks."

She was so pretty, and her smile so disarming, that Chang forgot his fear at once, and the two of them fell to laughing and joking together as if they had known each other all their lives. And so they continued for several hours, when unexpectedly a loud crashing noise came from the depths of the forest. Leaping to her feet, an expression of terror on her face, the girl cried, "One of my master's servants! I must flee!" Without another word she ran off into the thicket and disappeared.

Looking about in desperation and wondering what to do next, Chang decided to run for his boat. Before he could turn around there was a frightful hissing noise that made him freeze to the spot. There, slithering from the forest, and coming straight toward him was a great and hideous serpent with glowing eyes, dripping fangs, and a body as thick as a barrel. So huge was the monstrous thing that its tail was hidden in the depths of the foliage.

Petrified by his terror, Chang stood motionless — like a living statue. By the time he recovered his senses the serpent had twined itself around him, pinning him to a tree. Although he could hardly move, the young man was still able to breathe. When the terrible head of the serpent came looming toward his neck, its dreadful mouth gaping wide open, Chang nearly fainted.

With its needle-sharp fangs the serpent pierced Chang's throat ever so slightly. Chang could hardly feel a thing, but then he felt his life's blood begin trickling slowly and steadily to the ground. Dropping its head to the ground where the blood fell the snake began lapping it up with its long forked tongue. Chang knew that if he did not find a way of escaping very quickly he would die. He noticed that as the snake's head bobbed up and down it relaxed its grip around his middle. He was able to move one hand. That meant he had a slight chance to escape. In a pouch slung about his waist was a poison pill he had taken along as a protection should he be attacked by foxes or other wild beasts.

Carefully taking the pill from his pouch he threw it to the ground in the widening pool of blood at his feet.

The snake swallowed the pill in an instant. For a moment nothing happened, then it drew back its head, stiffened its body, and began swaying its head back and forth. It hissed furiously, crashing against the trees as it moved. Then it shuddered and trembled, writhing and hissing all the while. In so doing it loosened its grip, then uncoiled completely from Chang, who dragged himself away as quickly as he could move. He was light-headed and enfeebled from the loss of blood, but not too weak to stagger back to his boat from which he took a sword, and then returned to the edge of the forest. The mighty serpent lay there twitching, its ugly mouth slowly opening and closing. Brandishing his sword, Chang brought it down with a single powerful stroke, severing the snake's head from its body. Then lancing it with the point of his sword he bore it back to the boat as proof of his adventure.

The sun had long since set when Chang returned home. He fell unconscious to the sand when he set foot on the shore and had to be carried to his bed where he remained with a fever for a full thirty days. He recovered his health at the end of that time and, thereafter, whenever he spoke of his terrifying experience, he said that he was certain he had been captured by the snake because it first appeared to him in the captivating form of the beautiful girl.

# BYE-BYE, BABY

AS THE SUN DISAPPEARED and dusk gradually spread its blanket over the horizon, the wind began to blow. At first it was a gentle movement of the air, but before long it howled like some forlorn demon, rattling the shutters and the glass windowpanes. A full moon drifted in and out of misty, splotchy clouds, and its beams danced on the glistening snow until they were obscured by patches of black. It was during one of the periods of blackness that the thing appeared.

It seemed to come from nowhere, one moment the white hillside was deserted and the next it was violated by the hideous, slithering, dripping mass. It must have been very hot because thick, oily wisps of steam kept rising skyward as it inched its way toward the cabin. It did not seem to have any definite shape at first, just a formless glob that quivered as it moved, leaving behind a trail of ugly slime like that of a giant slug.

Inside the cabin two people waited, frozen with terror as they watched the monstrosity move closer and closer. The young woman wanted to scream, but the sounds were trapped in her throat, and she was forced to watch as though hypnotized. The man, suddenly awakened to the possibility of danger, rushed to the mantlepiece and grabbed the double-barreled shotgun, checking to make certain that it was loaded as he headed for the front door. The woman tried to stop him, but he refused to listen to her protests. Resolutely pushing her aside, he flung the door open and strode, coatless, into the bitter night.

Briefly he watched the Thing as it continued coming in his direction. Then, raising the shotgun to his shoulder, he took careful aim and fired both barrels. The roar of the two shotgun blasts echoed thunderously across the valley. The Thing shuddered slightly, then quivered to a stop. The man reloaded his weapon and waited, without taking his eyes off the monstrosity.

Then, as he stood waiting, a metamorphosis began to take place. The pellets had obviously affected the Thing. It began to shrink and change color. From a lifeless gray it turned green, then slid into blue, purple, red, and orange, and finally, a swirling, evanescent rainbow of luminous brilliance. Steam began to rise and a high-pitched whine filled the air, only to become a hiss that finally trailed off into inaudibility; steam and smoke surrounded the churning mass. Gradually the vapors drifted away revealing a figure in the snow. Approaching cautiously, the man stooped down to see what it was. He could hardly believe his eyes. There, not an arm's

19

length away, crumpled up in a melted depression in the snow, shivering convulsively, lay the most beautiful woman he had ever seen. She stirred at his approach and jumped back, cringing. Sitting up, she stared into his eyes with a penetrating look, her own eyes reflecting a combination of fear, curiosity, desire, and innocence. Unexpectedly, she stretched her hands toward him, and without thinking he seized them. Seeing that the girl was trembling violently, he gathered her up in his arms and turned back to the cabin. She clung to him tightly. The warmth of her body penetrated his clothing and deep within himself he felt a slightly uncomfortable tingling sensation. She kept her head on his shoulder and breathed, almost panted, in his ear. The trip back to the cabin seemed to take forever, but when they arrived he kicked the door open and hurried into the room with his unexpected burden.

The woman inside — his wife — fainted when she saw them.

Of course, the judge did not believe a word of the story that the husband told, all about the monstrosity, how it changed into a beautiful girl, etc. In fact, he reminded the man that it was overwhelming generosity on the part of the court that he was not committed to an institution or charged with perjury. The wife, too, denied the monster story. She said her husband had acted strangely, then gone outdoors and remained away for several hours. When she finally went to look for him, half beside herself with worry for his safety, she had found him with the girl — in a nice, warm, dry cave, hidden in the side of a hill. She would never have been able to find it (she explained) had it not been for the footprints in the snow. The judge was an old-fashioned man, and recommended a six months separation before they took any permanent steps.

The husband dropped out of sight shortly afterwards, the mysterious girl along with him. They turned up a year later, according to the report of a hunter who claimed to have seen them from a cabin in an isolated section of the High Sierras. He said that they were walking up a slope in the snow. He was watching them through binoculars because he thought they might be in trouble.

Then (continued the hunter) they paused about halfway up, and began to undress, even though it was about ten degrees below zero. They held hands and then they seemed to burst into a kind of flame, even brighter than the white of the snow, like Fourth of July fireworks, all different colors. When the smoke cleared away they had vanished.

Naturally, the hunter could not believe his eyes, but it was getting too cold and dark to go over to investigate. The next morning, he climbed up the slope to the exact spot where he had seen the fantastic sight the night before. It was easy to find because the snow all around had melted, then frozen over again into a smooth, glassy crust. Underneath was a pile of clothing. The hunter broke the ice and collected everything. There was no blood, nothing. But in a shirt pocket was a piece of paper all crumpled up. There were a few hard to read words scrawled on it. They seemed to say, "Bye-bye, baby. I'm sorry, but I couldn't help myself...." There was more, but it was completely illegible.

Later, when the paper was shown to the missing man's wife, she identified the handwriting as that of her husband. She cried after reading it, because, she said, he had always called her "baby" when he was worried, or didn't know what was going to happen next.

# THE PHANTOM BATTLE

THE SUMMER had almost come to an end, and Jeff could feel a crisp bite in the air that had not been present when he began his solitary cross-country bicycle trip. It ws nearly sundown and almost an hour had elapsed since he had last seen another human being, either in a car or by the roadside. It did not surprise him though, for he was in real wilderness. The only signs of civilization were the narrow asphalt two-lane road and the occasional pieces of refuse discarded unlawfully by mortorists.

He was getting more and more tired as he pedaled along, for it had been an uphill ride for the last several hours. Now, as he approached the pass ahead, he felt ready to drop. Not only was he tired, he was hungry and thirsty. The thought of the sandwiches in his back pack and the canteen full of tart limeade made his mouth water. Judging by the terrain, the nearest habitation was probably miles ahead in the valley beyond the pass. He did not want to wait that long before stopping.

Determined to go at least as far as the pass

itself, he pushed himself to the very limit of his endurance. Though his muscles ached and the heavy exertion at such high altitude made him light-headed, he mustered all his strength and finally succeeded in covering the final stretch. The sun had dropped behind a distant peak by the time he dismounted, and as he looked around the western sky was ablaze with brilliant streaks of scarlet, gold, and pink that gradually darkened at the eastern edges, presenting a distant wall of deep purple, blue, and black.

Standing there for a moment to gaze at the breathtaking panorama of sky, mountains, and misty valley below, Jeff knew that what he saw, except for the road, was exactly as it had been fifty, a hundred, even a thousand years ago, untouched, unspoiled by man or his works. Then, taking a deep breath, he seated himself on a huge smooth boulder with a chairlike depression in it. He settled back, opened his pack, and began unwrapping his sandwiches. Soggy and cold as they were, they looked better than a steak right now, and he attacked them vigorously. The scenery was so spectacular, the solitude so splendid, he completely lost himself in his daydreams. Soon he would be back in the bustling world of the university with the long hours and its rigid schedule of work and study. Shaking his head as if to dispel the idea, he leaned back against the rock and thought about the past several weeks of absolute freedom and carefree meandering to and from wherever the spirit had moved him.

How long he had been sitting there like this he did not know. Perhaps he even dozed off lightly. In any event, he suddenly started, sat up, and strained to peer out into the darkening shadows of the valley below. A distinct, but far-off hollow boom roused him from his sleepy state. "Oh, no," he thought. "Thunder, all I need up here is a rainstorm." But yet it did not quite sound like thunder, and although it was almost dark, the sky was quite clear, with a huge bright moon rising on the horizon. He listened again, this time with anxious anticipation. There was another boom followed by two more in rapid succession. It seemed illogical, impossible, but the sound reminded him of artillery fire. He had never heard the real thing, but he had certainly been exposed to enough of it on television and in the movies.

Climbing to his feet and looking sharply into the murky twilight, Jeff tried to determine the source of the rumbling booms, which now continued steadily in irregular tempo. He could see nothing, and then abruptly the noise stopped. The silence was heavy, not even the cry of a single night bird rang out. Abruptly the stillness was shattered by the unmistakable crackle of small-arms fire. The roar of the cannon burst forth again, louder than before, and the echoes of the bombardment reverberated through the mountains. Then, with a suddenness that defied all reason, the ear-shattering sounds of full battle exploded on all sides. From the swirling mists of the valley swarms of men emerged. Mounted cavalrymen thundered into view from nowhere. Wave after wave of infantrymen rose up from all sides. The shrill trumpeting of bugles mingled with neighing, screaming horses, the rumble and clatter of caissons on gravel, explosions, shrieks, curses, and shouts. Flattening himself against the rock, numb with shock, Jeff froze amidst the flash of bursting shells, flame-spurting rifle barrels, and the appalling, over-all spectacle of the violence around him. A squad of cavalrymen came clattering from behind him, their drawn sabers gleaming dully in the moonlight, blue sparks flying as the horses' hoofs struck the ground. Now the acrid smell of gunpowder reached his nostrils mingled with the overpowering stench of horses, sweat, and a sweet smell of decay.

Although he could scarcely believe his senses, it was impossible for him to deny the fact that he was in the midst of a battle so furious, so savage, it exceeded anything he had ever imagined. A loud snort accompanied by a terrible string of oaths made him look sharply over his left shoulder. Galloping toward him was a black-bearded rider in a tattered gray uniform. One leg was drenched with fresh blood that spread out over the saddle and belly of the horse. Brandishing a long, wicked-looking saber, the horseman fixed Jeff with a ferocious glare as he bore down, his face livid, his eyes glowing like smoldering embers.

Jerking his head aside so that the flashing sword missed him by a fraction of an inch,

Jeff yet heard the swish as it cut through the air. Then he scrambled behind the rock, panting, his heart pounding like a jackhammer.

The shrill whinnying of the horses, the roar of the cannon, the crackle of rifle fire, and the screams of the wounded and dying now blended together in a mind-bursting cacaphony of horror. There was nowhere to run, nowhere to hide. Now the thunder of hoofbeats and the clatter of wagon wheels crunching on gravel grew louder. In the pale light of the full moon Jeff could see with awful clarity the hordes of bedraggled men in blue and gray on both sides of the pass and all around him locked together in hand to hand combat. Hacking and spearing with bayonet and sword, blasting with pistol and rifle, grappling, throttling, stomping, and bludgeoning, they cursed and shouted as they fought like regiments of devils. The smoke and the dust and the stench were so overpowering that Jeff became sick to his stomach. For a moment or two only his own physical discomfort commanded his senses. Then, as he staggered away from the boulder, wiping his mouth with one sleeve and gasping for breath, he suddenly became aware that he was completely alone. Gone were the troopers, the horses, the cannon, the wagons. Gone were the terrible smells and sounds. The valley below was now completely blanketed in mist, and the pale moon above shone down on a solitary young man, shivering slightly as a fresh chill wind whipped spirals of dust around his ankles.

Trembling, he fastened the buttons of his faded blue denim jacket and walked over to where he had leaned his bicycle against a rock. He intended to ride until he came to a town if it took him all night. Then he noticed his rear tire was flat. "Oh, no!" he said aloud as he bent down to examine it. Taking a small flashlight from his pocket he examined the hole carefully. It looked as though it had been made by a large calibre bullet. As he stared in disbelief, his attention was drawn to a dark object at the edge of the light beam. There, half buried in the dirt, just beyond the hole in the tire was a bullet of exactly the right size ... but it looked old and was pitted and corroded. It had to have been there for at least a hundred years, maybe longer.

Looking back on his chilling experience later, Jeff realized that the uniforms and equipment of the fighting men he had seen were of the Civil War era. But there was no explanation for the phenomenon — unless what he had witnessed were the shades of some restless spectral warriors doomed to fight their dreadful battle at that pass for all eternity until granted their release from some higher power.

# THE JONAH

A HEAVY LAYER OF FOG blanketed the city, changing it into a silent, shrouded screen of slowly shifting gray shapes. The unnatural stillness was pierced from time to time by the lonely groan of distant foghorns that sounded like disembodied spirits, risen from the depths of the sea to sob their loneliness.

The young seaman turned up the collar of his pea coat, peered nervously over his shoulder, and lowered his seabag to the sidewalk. He could not see beyond the pale yellowish glow of the streetlight. He was completely alone, yet, somewhere not far away out there in the swirling fog, the footsteps kept coming. He had made up his mind to stop and take his chances. All he had in his pocket were a few dollars, an assignment slip for his next berth, and a switchblade knife. He backed up against the lamppost and nervously tightened his fingers around the handle of the knife. If only he had been able to find pier 17 ... but he was lost and scared. He knew only too well what could happen to a stranger along the waterfront at night in a thick fog.

He cocked his head and listened. The footsteps were coming closer now. His heart beat faster. *Calm down,* said a silent voice inside his head. *Maybe it will be someone who can give you directions.*

Clutching the cord of his seabag with one hand and the knife with his other he waited, every muscle in his body tense and alert. Gradually he began to distinguish the outlines of a figure emerging from the screening fog, and then he found himself face to face with an older man, who by his dress seemed to be a ship's officer. The officer's eyes were an ice-cold blue and the stubble of several days' beard bristled from his face, giving it the appearance of being covered with frost. His skin was leathery.

The young seaman was overcome with relief. He let go of the knife and said, " 'Scuse me, sir, could you tell me how to get to pier 17?"

The older man's face remained expressionless. "Are you signing on the old *Foxfire?*"

"As a matter of fact, I am. Are you a crew member?"

Instead of answering, the man said, "I wouldn't ship out on her if I was you."

"Why?"

30

"There's a Jonah on board her, that's why."

The young man smiled. "Oh, come on, now. Nobody believes in that sort of stuff anymore. Men don't carry bad luck around with them like seabags."

"That's what you believe, eh?"

The seaman was about to answer, but something held him back. The older man pointed a long, weather-beaten finger at him and continued. "I'm going to tell you something, mister, and I promise, you'll never forget it. . . . " The mournful sound of a foghorn interrupted him, then faded into the stillness. He kept speaking as if he had never heard a thing. "Exactly twenty years ago this very night the *Foxfire* was a day out of Liverpool, bound for Suez by way of Marseilles. She was just abeam of the Scilly Isles when a gale blew down from the Irish Sea and the skipper had to change course to keep her from foundering in the trough. Well, sir, there was another ship nearby, a Hog Islander out of Boston bound for Swansea to pick up a load of coal. Her name was the *Rocket*. She got blown off course and piled up on the rocks, and started sending out an S.O.S.

"Now, it just so happened that the *Foxfire* was the nearest ship. She was the logical one to come to the rescue . . . could have made it in five hours, even in heavy seas."

"You mean . . ."

"I mean she never changed course. Her

31

skipper was carrying a cargo under a bare-boat charter. If he didn't reach his last port by a certain time he was going to have to pay a penalty."

"Then what happened to the *Rocket?*"

The older man lowered his voice. "She was battered to pieces by the waves and went down with all hands."

"I ... I'm sorry to hear that."

"Not as sorry as the women and children of those crewmen were when they heard the news. . . . But they weren't the only ones who heard. The sea keeps some things secret, but not all things."

"I don't understand."

"Bad news gets around. By the time the *Foxfire* got to Marseilles every man on board knew what their skipper had done. Half of them signed off the ship then and there. The rest at the other ports along the way. They were smart. Things started happening aboard the *Foxfire*. A man fell from the crosstrees and got killed. A boiler blew up in the engine room. Oh, it was one thing after another. Pretty soon word got around that there was a Jonah on board. It was the skipper himself. Before that voyage ended, men began seeing strange things. Lights that weren't there. Misty figures on the fo'csle head at night. Wet footprints on deck. Green slime and seaweed in bunks ... It was the dead crewmen of the *Rocket*. Some said they were looking for revenge, others said they were just trying to get home. Well, sir, whatever anybody thought about it, everybody knew something was wrong . . . especially the skipper. He started to drink. And by the time they got back to their home port . . . this one, as a matter of fact, he couldn't get himself a job as skipper of a garbage scow."

"So what happened to him after that?"

"He kept going down, down, down. Then he disappeared. Word had it that he'd died. But it wasn't so. He stowed away in the shaft alley of a tanker bound for the Persian Gulf. When her skipper heard his story after they found him, he was signed on as an ordinary seaman. It was a mistake. One night when he was standing lookout on the midnight-to-four watch he heard a queer sound like a chorus of sighs. He turned around and thought he was done for, because there, climbing up over the railing of the wing of the bridge, were seven green slimy men. Their eyes glowed like coals out of hell itself, they were covered with barnacles, and their hair was tangled with seaweed. He tried to move but he couldn't. He tried to cry out, but he couldn't open his mouth. Well, they grabbed him with their cold slimy hands, but with grips like steel. Now he knew he was finished . . . that is he thought he knew. Trouble was, he didn't know what they really had in store for him. No sir! They held him there till the rest of their dead shipmates came, climbing and squishing, and dripping slime all over the deck. They overpowered the helmsman of that tanker and they steered straight for the rocks off the Strait of Hormuz. They struck before dawn and the tanker went down with all hands . . . . except for the ex-skipper of the *Foxfire*. The dead crewmen of the *Rocket* put him in a raft, and before they sank back down to Davy Jones' Locker the dead captain pointed a long bony finger, and spoke in a horrible voice that gurgled like a drowning man sir fathoms down:

'Now hear this, Jeremy Samsel [that was his name], for twenty years you'll sail the seas a despised and lonely man. Seamen and landlubbers alike will shun you like the plague. You will be a wanderer without a home port, you will be a sailor without a berth — a Jonah, hated and feared wherever you go. Ashore we'll come to you in the night and cover you with slime and trouble your sleep till you go mad with terror. At sea we'll crouch in the dark just under the waves, and wait for your ship to drive her to the rocks, or drag her to the bottom. There will be no rescue for your shipmates, they'll all go down the way you let us go down, without a chance, without hope. . . . Then twenty years from now you'll sign on the *Foxfire* again wherever she is, wherever you may be. And then, on the first midnight watch after she leaves port, we'll all rise up from the sea and hold a hearing of the dead to pass final judgement on you.'

"And then they sank down into the sea again, leaving him there alone on the raft, trembling like a loose hawser in a hurricane."

"Now just hold on there, mister," said the young seaman, peering into the stranger's face. "You don't expect me to believe wild sea stories like that, do you?"

The man's face clouded. "No," he replied thoughtfully. "I don't suppose I do. But then, there's a way you can find out for yourself, isn't there?"

"What do you mean?"

The older man smiled mirthlessly. "You don't have to follow my advice. Nobody's stopping you from signing on the *Foxfire*. She sails tomorrow, you know. You'd know for sure by the first midnight watch after that, wouldn't you?"

In the distance a foghorn sounded again, and somewhere nearby the young seaman thought he could hear the sound of seven ships bells signifying eleven-thirty, just half an hour before midnight. Without thinking, he turned in the direction he thought he had heard the bells coming from, and at that moment a slight breeze came up, cutting through the fog like a giant, unseen broom. There, not a hundred feet away was a pier, its faded lettering barely visible in the dim light. Pier 17, it said, and beyond loomed the shrouded outlines of an ungainly, rust-covered ship, the *Foxfire*.

The young seaman turned back to his companion and started to say, "Hey, you knew . . ." but he stopped himself in mid-sentence. He was as alone as he had been when he first approached the streetlight. The breeze died down again and the fog closed in once more around the pier across the way. He squinted and strained to see where the man had gone, but there wasn't a sign of him . . . except that where he had been standing was a puddle of water edged in green slime and a few strands of seaweed.

# THE FULFILLMENT

*This is the way the world ends*
*Not with a bang but a whimper.*
from "The Hollow Men" *by T.S.*
*Eliot*

FOR YEARS tension had been mounting. Daily, the newspapers screamed in blaring headlines that the critical nature of world affairs spelled impending disaster. In churches the clergy continually urged congregations to pray for peace. Politicians blamed other politicians, who shook their fists, glared back, and replied in kind. The Rightists screamed at the Leftists and the Leftists screamed back at the Rightists, meanwhile both, in their respective parts of the world, calmly continued building intercontinental ballistic missiles with nuclear warheads.

When winds were favorable, and H-bombs stamped "Made in U.S.A." "Made in the U.S.S.R." "Made in France," or "Made in the People's Republic of China," pulverized remote islands or mountains, the only rumble heard in New York or London or Moscow was that of subway trains endlessly speeding. Anxious watchers scanned the skies, but no foreign missiles appeared. In some quarters people whispered that the weather was slowly being changed by so many nuclear blasts, and a rumor even started once that the very atmosphere of the Earth had started to leak away into space — and that sending men and machines to the moon would only hasten the process. Now and again a few people would panic and wind up in mental institutions, but the atmosphere clung resolutely to the Earth, mankind continued to breathe, and most of the nations finally signed a nuclear test ban treaty.

Periodically there appeared in the press stories about scattered suicides blamed on despondency over the world situation, and in the upper echelons of the United Nations there was a growing concern over violence and terrorism, and conditions in Africa, Asia, and the Middle East. Every night people in Chicago, Liverpool, Leningrad, and Bordeaux would shake their heads at the news, then go home and watch television till their eyes turned red. But no cataclysm befell mankind.

When an editor in middle America said that Russia was threatening world peace by stepping up the Soviet missile program, people worried. The Russians countered with the usual accusation that Western imperialism was leading the world down a one-way path to war. Still no catastrophe happened.

Springs gave way to summers, and babies kept being born. Satellites continued rising from both East and West. Occasional tensions were relieved when former enemies licked their wounds and shook hands. Tears and

38

blood flowed when neighbors became enemies and killed one another. Hollywood, London, Paris, and Rome discovered that horror movies made great profits, and the public spent huge sums of money for the privilege of cringing in the dark, safe, yet terrified. An old man said, "The pennydreadfuls are back, but now they cost three dollars." And the second-rate movie houses introduced film buffs to a future proving mutants and robots to be even more sinister than crooked politicians and knife-wielding junkies.

The status quo prevailed, however, and life continued to go on as it always had. When truly strange things actually happened, they were catalogued away in dusty files along with yesterday's flying-saucer stories. The wonderful and terrible part about it was that the peculiar events were so thoroughly commonplace that no one bothered to wonder about them at all. A little girl in Northern Canada told about a bear who asked her funny questions, but those who heard her story either shrugged in disbelief or laughed it off as a whimsical joke. In any event they soon forgot.

One dark night in San Francisco a cat fell from an office window breaking its neck. Death was instantaneous. It was a nondescript beast, and had it been discovered the carcass would have been dumped in the nearest trashcan. But it was never found for, seconds after touching the ground, the limp little bundle of fur and bones was seized by the powerful talons of an eagle and whisked off into the night air. The bird then winged its way to a distant aerie, far from the prying eyes of man, and a puzzled electronic designer never understood how a tiny container of microfilm had disappeared. Nothing had changed, no one was suspicious, and everything continued according to plan.

Not a person in Pittsburgh or Milan ever heard about this and, if they had, most likely they would have merely shrugged and continued about their business. But in Bombay, a fakir lay dead on a narrow, dingy back street, his flute silent beside him, his basket empty. What would have appeared most unusual were the fang marks precisely over the carotid arteries — coupled to the fact that the body had been drained of all its blood. But nobody saw these things and no one bothered to investigate, for death has a familiar face in India. Somewhere in the city a thing resembling a fat cobra slithered silently and swiftly toward a destination in the Harischandra hills.

Some occurrences did not go unnoticed, but they remained mysteries and were soon forgotten. For several days there was great excitement in a plant that refined uranium isotopes somewhere in the Soviet Union. Several ounces of valuable fissionable material had disappeared. There was a rapid investigation, several equally rapid trials and executions, and no publicity. The material was never recovered and several tourists in the district complained bitterly that their luggage had been rifled. In Florida a honeymoon couple disappeared. It was assumed that they had gone on a moonlight swim and drowned, but no one ever really learned what had happened. Vandals were blamed when several museums and libraries were broken into and robbed. A few politicians enhanced their images by clamoring for crackdowns on crime and vice, but of course the culprits were never caught and nothing really changed. Once there was a great uproar when an airliner vanished without a trace. Most of the time these disappearances, thefts, and deaths were attributed to carelessness, racial tensions, drug addicts, or terrorists. In some quarters there were fearful whisperings about vampires, ghosts, and other evil spirits, but these rumors were ridiculed by all but the true believers.

A Montana writer with a very vivid imagination, who was a devotee of the works of Charles Fort, became curious about these seemingly unconnected happenings. He wrote an article on the subject and suggested that there was a thread of continuity. He even offered a theory that these events were not isolated, but were indeed part of some mysterious single effort. He went on to suggest that this effort might be extraterrestrial in nature. He suggested that the Earth was being studied, dissected by some unseen, unknown visitors who were alien to this planet. He wrote:

*It is not outside the realm of possibility that
some cautious visitors from outer space are
making a careful, painstaking study of Earth
and everything on it. When this survey is completed, and their data interpreted, they may
contact the human race.*

The article was quite detailed and highly doc-
umented with odd news items gleaned from
the world press. It provided extremely fascinating reading and was published by a leading science-fiction magazine. It was given
considerable attention by many of the readers
and created a controversy that did wonders
for circulation. Naturally, those who de-
nounced the article, did so vigorously. Again
the controversy flared up, and again circulation increased. The editors were so pleased
that they assigned the writer a whole series
on the subject. Unfortunately, the day after
he received the good news he was clawed and
mauled to death by a grizzly bear. The arti-
cles were never written, and the controversy,
like so many others, died down and was forgotten.

The great cities of the Earth are magnificent monuments to the achievements of man
down through the ages. The palaces and
cathedrals of Europe, the golden temples of
Asia, the great works of art, and the mighty
skyscrapers of America all give mute testi-
mony to his greatness. The intricate machines built by the last men to make their life

more comfortable and secure proved man's genius. The great talents he developed enabled him to wrest the richest treasures from the very heart of the Earth. With his brain and his hands he accomplished feats which would have stunned his ancestors. He created a fabulous wonderland out of the splendid, savage wilderness into which he was born. He surpassed the ability of the birds to fly and the fishes to swim. He burrowed deeper beneath the Earth's surface than any other of her creatures. He was able to hurl his voice and his image completely around the planet at will. He even began to force secrets from the sun, the moon, and the stars. He chained the forces of electricity and made them seem puny next to the might of the tiny atom, whose awesome energies he unleashed and ultimately made do his bidding.

He was civilized and wild, he was good and evil. He was lord over all the creatures of the Earth, and yet, he was always part of them. Despite his wisdom and strength he often succumbed to those weaker than himself, and to the end he respected even the microbe. He was a living paradox, this creature, man, because at times he fancied himself invincible, yet to the very last a spark of humility burned within him. We honor and respect the memory of man, and we weep over his fate, but we were never destined to live with him, for he would have destroyed us had he known of us.

When first our powerful thought beams

spanned the vastness of the universe and we came upon man, we trembled, for we feared that one day he might discover our secrets, then seek us out and annihilate us. Nevertheless, we hoped that some day he might mature, that we could reveal ourselves to him, that we might live together in harmony. But that day never came. We grew more fearful when we found that we could not enter man's mind and prepare him for our coming. Though we succeeded with a few individuals the experiment was a failure, and those who attained the true cosmic consciousness were destroyed by it. We were sorrowful, for we did not wish to see this magnificent creature perish, but we had no choice, for the will to survive is stronger than compassion. Thus we took possession of the lesser creatures. We moved on the stealthy foot of the cat, the fleet wing of the bird, and with the sinewy muscle of the serpent. Through the eyes of these beasts we saw, and through their ears we heard. We wept for those who were slashed by the claw or pierced by the fang, for like man we know emotion, but unlike man we have abhorred violence.

For many centuries we studied, collected, and absorbed Earth's knowledge. We were ever on the alert lest we be discovered. Always we hoped against hope that we might some day gain access to the ultimate, to the minds of all men before it was too late. Only as a last resort did we wish to unleash the nameless force against which there is no defense, which could swiftly, silently, painlessly eradicate an entire species from the universe. Our goal of saving man we could not attain, for his salvation was beyond even our power. Finally, then, as man fumbled to open the lock guarding the secrets of the mind, our peril became too great and man unwittingly sealed his own doom. Unfalteringly, proudly, and blindly he strode down the path that led him into the twilight of his day, then to the endless night of oblivion.

Now the twinkling lights of New York are out and the streets lie hushed and empty. The wind whistles and moans through the cables of the Golden Gate bridge, but no brightly colored automobiles scurry across its span. For San Francisco is a dead city that lies still, save for the cries of the sea gulls wheeling and spinning in lazy circles over the seven silent hills. The Metro no longer rumbles beneath Paris as the leaves flutter endlessly down the Champs Elysées, and in the Eternal City of Rome ancient statues brood mutely over past glories while pigeons roost on cafe tables along the Via Veneto. In London, Big Ben chimes no more, and there are none to listen except for those who slumber beneath marble slabs in Westminster Abby, who have passed beyond time.

But the cherry blossoms still bloom on the banks of the Potomac, and at the foot of Mount Fuji, and the oranges grow ripe in the green groves of Valencia. The deer walks fearlessly through the empty streets of Denver, and the she-wolf sleeps peacefully with her cubs in the silent halls of the Kremlin.

And with the secrets we have digested from the wisdom of man we shall abandon our dark and murky planet, and soon migrate to this bright and peaceful place with its misty waterfalls, its green lands, its blue seas, and its sweet clean air — and one of man's oldest prophecies will finally be fulfilled as we, who are named The Meek, shall inherit the Earth.

# THE TOAD THING

A CHILL WIND kicked dust up along the roadside as the two boys trudged away from town.
They had hoped to spend the night there, but
had failed to find a place to stay. As it was,
they were lucky not to be locked up as va-
grants. The locals, with disapproving eyes
and downturned mouths, had no use for out-
of-state youths with long hair, sprouting
beards, and backpacks.

Neither of them spoke as they headed wea-
rily down the road, but both felt a growing
uneasiness at having to sleep outside in such
gloomy, inhospitable country. They both
heard the gurgling of water at about the
same time, and they quickened their pace in
hopes of reaching it before darkness enveloped them completely. Somehow, the thought
of spending the night alongside a brook or
creek seemed safer, more comfortable than
staying in the woods or in a barren field.

The gurgling sound came from a heavily
wooded area off to the right of the road and
they hurried into the thicket, hoping to reach

their destination before dark. Fortunately the foliage was not too dense, and in ten minutes time they came to a clearing. The gurgling and splashing was much louder now, and for good reason. There before them was a small pond with a waterfall at one end. The drop was a short one, hardly more than five feet. It was what they saw at the opposite end of the pond that intrigued them. There, silhouetted against the purpling sky, was the unmistakable outline of an old house.

They could see upon closer examination that it was old, abandoned, and crumbling with rot and age. The side facing the pond was slightly lopsided, giving the impression that it was about to collapse into the water. This was partly due to the fact that protruding from the wall was an old broken mill wheel. It hung there at an angle, looking as though the slightest touch would knock it to pieces.

"Are we in luck," crowed Tom, the older of the two. "We can sleep in there."

"I don't know," replied Dan, his companion. "The place gives me the creeps."

"What's the matter? You chicken?"

" 'Course not, but I still say the place is creepy looking."

"Maybe so, but if it started to rain, I'd rather sleep in there than out here."

"I think I'd rather get wet."

"Don't you at least want to check it out first?"

Dan sighed. "Okay, if you insist."

Conversation over, they approached the old house and cautiously tried the door. The hinges were so rusty that it took both their efforts to pull it open. The lock was long since gone. The moment they entered, a dank, musty smell assailed them, and the cold penetrating dampness made them shiver unexpectedly, although neither would admit it to the other.

Tom took out a flashlight and scanned the room with its beam. The place was festooned with cobwebs. Spiders and other little creatures scurried away as if in sudden panic. The two young men shivered again.

"Have you seen enough?" asked Dan.

"That's a pretty dumb question. We've only been in this room. Come on."

Instead of answering, Dan took out his own flashlight and flicked it on. Slowly they moved from one dilapidated room to another, taking pains to avoid rotten spots in the creaking floor boards, until they had covered the entire house, from top to bottom. In some of the rooms broken pieces of furniture still remained. The kitchen had an ancient fireplace, a wooden sink, and a rusty pump, while the upper rooms still had the crumbling remains of beds and mattresses which now looked as though they housed families of rats. Ugly green fungus growths made slimy splotches on the walls and jagged slivers of filthy glass stuck precariously out around the edges of several windows.

Recognizing that the only safe and sensible

place to sleep would be the kitchen, provided they could build a fire, they set to work clearing out a space in which to stretch out their sleeping bags. They then investigated the fireplace. Fortunately for them the chimney was not blocked and before long they had a roaring fire going. This was good, because the batteries in their flashlights had begun to wear out and they had no other means of illumination.

Night had fallen and beyond the abandoned house the darkness was absolute. There was no moon and the clouds that had been gathering all evening blotted out the stars. Aside from the crackling of the fire and the continuous splashing of the water outside there were no sounds of life. Although neither boy would admit it to the other there was something about the place that was terribly depressing. Normally the two were talkative and cheerful. Now each found it impossible to choose the right words for conversation. Tom had a small transistor radio, but when he tried to play it, all it gave out was a stream of crackling static.

"What will we do when the fire dies out?" murmured Dan softly.

"Sleep. What else?"

"I wish we could keep it going all night."

"Then go get some more wood, I don't care. . . . I don't know about you, Dan, but I'm gonna eat first. I'm starved."

That was when they heard the creaking. It was slow and distinct, like someone trying to open a door without being observed, but failing because it had been stuck for too long a time. It was an ominous creak that sent chills down the spine, and both boys froze as they listened.

"Tom! Did you hear it?"

Dan did not get an answer because at that moment there came a loud crash that sounded like the slamming of a door. It seemed to come from beneath the floor.

"Why don't you take a look in the next room," suggested Tom.

"I'm not going out there alone. You can if you want to, but I'm staying right here."

"Now that's just plain stupid! Okay, if that's the way you want it, I'll go and see for myself."

"Don't do it, Tom . . . I . . . I've got a funny feeling. . . ."

"Just cool it. I'll be right back."

Taking up his flashlight, Tom got to his feet and left the kitchen. Dan's heart began to pound. Despite the warmth of the fire he felt an icy chill grip him, and along with it the most sudden, unreasonable terror he had ever known. It overcame him like an explosion. His teeth began chattering and his hands trembled violently. He wanted to run from the room and join Tom, but he felt too weak to move.

Peering through the darkness of the room beyond he tried to see what, if anything, his companion had found. He could hear Tom's footsteps and could get glimpses of his flash-

light beam. It had grown dim, but was far
from being out altogether. Tom was out of
sight now, and the yellowish finger of light
from his flashlight swept the darkness slowly.
That was when Dan saw it. Blurry and indistinct, like a hulking man lurching from the
shadows, a figure appeared for a moment in
the waning light beam and was gone. But it
was crazy. Dan could have sworn that it had
a head like some giant, ugly, bulging-eyed
toad.

"Tom!" he cried. "Tom! Did you see . . ."

His question was answered by the most
bloodcurdling screams he had ever heard, followed by the horrible crashing and thrashing
of what sounded like a life and death struggle. Overcoming his terror, Dan scooped up
his own flashlight and ran into the next room,
where he tripped on something and fell to the
floor. The flashlight flew from his hand,
struck something, and went black. Thinking
only about recovering it, he groped about on
the filthy, littered floor. His hand closed on
something. . . .

"Aggghh!" he yelled, pulling his hand back
from the soft furry body of a rat. Squealing
in protest the rodent lashed about and
squirmed loose, scurrying off into the darkness. In the distance there was a loud slam,
like a heavy door closing. Then silence.

The cold chill of terror was gone now, but
in its place came concern for his friend.
"Tom!" he cried. "Where are you? Tom!
Are you okay?" The only answer was the

gurgling of the water outside. No longer did the fire in the kitchen crackle; it had almost burned out and the embers were now a dull glow in the grate.

His heart pounding with excitement, Dan reached in his pocket and took out a book of matches. He struck one and held it high. There in the far corner of the room was his flashlight. Sighing with relief, he rushed over and picked it up. He tried the switch. It worked. Thank God! he thought; then he gathered a few scraps of wood to take back for the fire.

Once the fire was going again Dan debated with himself. Should he or should he not go looking for Tom? Gathering up all his courage he decided he had to try. Remembering a wreck of a four-poster bed in one of the rooms upstairs, he plunged through the darkness, up the creaky stairs, and into the musty room. Seizing one of the bedposts he tugged till it broke away. Then, brandishing it like a club, he checked all the rooms on the top floor. Finding no trace of his friend, he cautiously descended to the kitchen.

He was about to start investigating the ground floor, room by room, when something made him freeze. It was the same creaking sound he had heard just before Tom disappeared. Tightening his grip on the broken bedpost he strained to listen. The creaking had stopped, but now he heard the footsteps. They were heavy, clumping, dragging sounds and they seemed to be coming from the same place as had the creaking, probably a cellar. Louder and closer they came. He backed up toward the fireplace. Without warning the terrible chill overcame him again. Cold sweat broke out on his forehead. His knees turned to soft plastic and he began trembling so hard all over that he could hardly keep from biting his tongue.

Now, as the heavy steps grew louder, he could hear the creaking of stairs. Remembering the stairs beyond the kitchen, Dan summoned up all his strength and raised his flashlight, aiming it into the black emptiness. He could barely see the top of the staircase. There was no doubt in his mind that from the shadows below something was coming up. The beam of the flashlight had grown so dim he could barely distinguish anything beyond five or six feet away. The footsteps grew louder. In between he could hear a hoarse, gurgly, heavy breathing. Terror turned to panic because there, emerging from the blackness, just beyond the fading beam of the flashlight, was the faint outline of something . . . something like the head of a giant toad. It was blurry and indistinct. But as it rose up it seemed to be atop the body of a lumpy, misshapen human figure.

The light went dead, and in the flickering yellow shadows cast by the fire in the kitchen it was impossible to see anything clearly. The short, gasping breaths were punctuated by heavy footsteps now. In final desperation, Dan threw the useless flashlight in the direction of the figure, then without looking back dashed toward the front door with all the determination of one who knows that death is at his heels.

Inhaling lungsful of fresh air Dan ran headlong into the thick underbrush of the land that lay between the old house and the road. Twisted branches became bony fingers tearing at his clothes, ripping at his flesh, pulling at his hair. With his eyes tightly shut and his arms outstretched, he plunged ahead, no longer able to think, and barely able to feel the pain of the abrasions and bruises that now covered his arms and face.

Suddenly his right foot hit something slippery and he lost his balance. Pitching forward, his arms and legs flailing wildly, he rolled down a steep incline. Then, a thousand bright lights exploded in his head and he vanished into nothingness.

When consciousness returned Dan found himself in a strange bed in unfamiliar surroundings. His head hurt. In fact as he looked around he realized that he ached all over. He tried to sit up but he couldn't. He tried to say something but his voice was gone. Tears welled up in his eyes and a tightness constricted his chest as he struggled for speech. Then he heard a voice. It came from an elderly man who stood at the foot of the bed. He wore a pale blue, faintly military looking trousers and shirt. A star was pinned over his pocket.

"Just like the last one that strayed out t'the

old mill after dark. Only *he's* lucky, all he's lost is his voice. . . ." He paused and looked directly into Dan's eyes. "You hear me, boy?" he asked. Dan nodded affirmatively. "Good. The doc says you're gonna be okay. Got yerself a couple of bad scratches and a powerful big lump on the head, but you'll be all right in a few days. You just get some rest now."

"You do like the sheriff says," declared the nurse softly. "Just try to sleep now."

He hadn't noticed her before. She was standing alongside the bed and slightly behind him to the right. He could tell now that he was in a hospital. The awareness of it reassured him and he closed his eyes again.

Just as they had told him, in a few days he was well enough to leave. He could walk and talk, his scratches were healed, and his bruises fading. There were fresh clothes waiting for him and a one-way ticket back home. He was just as glad to be on his way — more so, probably — than they were to see him go. Only one thing bothered him. It would bother him for the rest of his life. What had really happened to Tom? Dan was sure he would never know. The sheriff's explanation that Tom had probably fallen into a patch of quicksand alongside the pond while looking for firewood simply did not ring true.

Could there be anything to the fantastic tale that the old man from the local mortuary had told him, that the old mill was haunted by the restless spirits of a man, his wife, and their misshapen, half-witted son. They had

56

been reputed to waylay unsuspecting passers-by, murder them, and toss their bodies into a pit of quicksand through a trap door in the cellar after robbing them of their worldly possessions? Dan might have dismissed the whole thing as nonsense had it not been for one thing — the old man's description of the half-wit as an ugly, hulking blob of a creature with a head like a great, malignant, popeyed toad.

# THE BARGAIN

IF ANYONE were to mention Roddy Abel's name today, all they would probably get would be a blank stare or a puzzled frown along with the question, "Roddy who?" But the fact of the matter is he was the hottest deejay in show business ten years ago. All he had to do was play a record once and it was assured of being a hit — selling at least a million copies. Lord, was that man popular!

Women fell all over themselves just to get him to smile at them. Girls screamed and stampeded just to be near him, to touch his sleeve and maybe tear off a button or a thread. Even the men and boys weren't immune. He could hit a ball as well as a major leaguer, he was one of the best amateur stock-car racers in the field, his perforamce in the bowling alley made professionals wish he had stayed on the golf course, where even champions paled when they heard he was coming to play.

Of course, it wasn't always like that with him. In fact, until he first started doing his sensational *Roddy's Party* show, that every-

one mispronounced as *Roddy's Poddy* nobody had ever heard of him. There had been
no reason to, either.

Roddy had been a rich kid — or so he
thought — who was brought up by an uncle
who was supposed to be worth millions.
Roddy didn't do badly actually, until just
after he was graduated from college. But
then, unexpectedly, the uncle died. Two cousins appeared out of the woodwork with a bat-
tery of determined lawyers, and the battle
was on. When the smoke cleared away Roddy
was out in the street with nothing but a couple of suitcases full of clothes and the fading
remnants of the previous summer's tan.

He had been a real playboy in school; figur-
ing that he would eventually get his uncle's
money, he had never acquired any real skills.
He hadn't started racing yet, and apparently,
at the time, he wasn't good enough in the
other sports to become a professional. Who
knows, maybe the idea never occurred to him.
All anyone can do is guess now.

Anyway, in the beginning he had a few
dollars — enough to rent a cheap room in a
sleazy rooming house and keep him for a few
weeks while he looked for a job. Roddy's
chief problem was not so much that he
couldn't really do anything. He was a snob.
He could have gotten a job waiting on tables,
or washing dishes, or selling door-to-door.
There are lots of jobs that aren't particularly
appealing because they aren't glamorous and
require hard work, but they're honest and
can keep a person alive. Well, Roddy had

never had to look at things that way before, and the next thing he knew he only had one suit of clothes left, no suitcases, no watch, no place to live, and no money — except for an old 1875 silver dollar that he swore he would never part with as long as he lived.

He began sleeping in subways and on buses. He made it a point, however, to look as neat as he could, so that when he went up to a stranger on the street near a bus stop, or a phone booth, or a subway station, he could always say in that polished Ivy League accent of his, "This is awfully embarrassing, but I don't seem to have anything smaller than a five, could you possibly lend me a dime . . . . I'll be glad to give you my card, and I'll send it back to you the first thing in the morning."

He knew exactly what kind of people to approach. He knew they would never miss a dime, and it always worked. He didn't make a lot, but he generally managed to clear fifteen to twenty-five dollars a day. So for a while he was able to afford another cheap room. But then he started to spend too much of his spare time drinking — all he had was spare time — and after a few months he was drinking up more than he could collect a dime at a time. Now he raised the ante and began asking for a quarter, a half-dollar. For a while it worked, but one day he picked the wrong man, and the next thing he knew he was being booked for vagrancy at the nearest precinct station.

He had been drinking — not much, just

enough to be nasty — and by the time he had sobered up sufficiently to realize what trouble he was in, Roddy found himself being locked up in a cell for the night. Well, he pleaded guilty the next day, and since he didn't have any previous record, the judge gave him a suspended sentence.

The day was a gloomy one in late November. All the stores were decorated with turkeys and pumpkins for Thanksgiving. Roddy had probably never felt so low in his life. He was cold. He was broke. He had a police record. And he needed a shave. With his hands thrust deep in his pockets he walked and walked, feeling sorrier and sorrier for himself as time passed.

It was just about lunch hour when he found himself in front of the public library at Forty-Second Street and Fifth Avenue. He felt frozen to the marrow by this time and since he didn't have enough money for lunch, he decided to go inside and warm up. He could always fill himself up and temporarily assuage the hunger pangs by drinking from the water fountains. He turned and started climbing the steps leading to the main entrance when suddenly he felt a hand on his arm. He was so startled that he jumped as he spun around.

"Oh, excuse me," apologized an elderly man in a dark, nondescript suit. "I didn't mean to upset you. It's just that I don't know my way around the library. Do you know where the books on the supernatural are?"

Roddy's initial reaction ordinarily might

have been one of arrogance, but something about the man made him restrain himself. During his student days he had spent many hours in the library's reading rooms, and he knew his way around it quite well. Instead of being rude, he offered to show the old man where the main catalogue was, and for his pains, to his profound delight, the man invited him to lunch. Ah, thought Roddy to himself, maybe my luck is changing.

Over lunch Roddy Abel and the elderly stranger talked of many things. The conversation began with the subject of the supernatural. It went from ghosts and demons and haunts to vampires, werewolves, witchcraft, black magic. Then abruptly the man changed the subject. Leaning forward on the table he fixed Roddy with a penetrating stare and said, "You're a very unhappy young man, aren't you."

It was a statement, not a question, and it took Roddy so by surprise, that he suddenly found himself pouring out his soul to this man he had never seen in his life. All the bitterness and venom and anger boiled up and flowed out until he had laid himself bare.

After taking it all in the old man smiled knowingly, leaned back, and said, "You've learned the truth, haven't you? There is no such thing as justice. To be right doesn't necessarily mean that you will win, does it?"

"How well I know," replied Roddy bitterly.

"Then you agree with me that the most important things in the world are wealth and power."

"Agree!" exclaimed Roddy, clenching his fists and narrowing his eyes. "I would sell myself body and soul ... I would forfeit the rest of my life for a year or two of all the wealth and power I wanted!"

The old man chuckled. "You're young, my friend. Why, in a year or even two, you could barely begin. In your case I would suggest ten at least."

By now Roddy was convinced that the old man was half-mad, but he had bought a lavish lunch. He was entitled to his little games.

"I'd take ten gladly," Roddy declared.

"Shall we make a bargain, then?" asked the old man.

"Why not," answered Roddy, offering his hand.

Their hands clasped across the table. Roddy felt a sudden tingling in his whole body. It was as though he had grabbed a live wire and could not let go. For an instant, only the briefest of instants, the stranger's eyes seemed to glow with an inner fire. Then he smiled, withdrew his hand, and said softly, "Ten years, then." With that he got up and left without saying another word.

For a moment Roddy just sat there, half cursing himself for letting the old man make a fool of him, half pleased at having managed to get himself a free meal. As he got up from the table and headed for the door the cold clear light of reality returned, reminding him that he had no idea of where his next meal would come from, or where he would spend the night.

Although he didn't know it at that precise moment, it was a problem he would never have to face again as long as he lived.

The realization hit him just before he stepped outside the restaurant door into the street. He happened to glance over at the front page of a newspaper that a man was reading there. Staring out at him almost as big as life were the faces of his two cousins — the ones who had cheated him out of his inheritance. MILLIONAIRE BROTHERS KILLED IN AUTO CRASH read the headline. Roddy could hardly believe it. The pictures and the print began to grow fuzzy before his eyes as they filled with tears — tears of joy and triumph. They were the only ones between him and the money that had been rightfully his, and now they were gone. He knew exactly what to do next.

It is doubtful that Roddy Abel gave much thought to the elderly man who bought him lunch on the day he learned he was to be rich again. From that day on his life was a whirlwind of excitement — fast expensive cars, beautiful girls, applause, and power. A word from Roddy Abel in the right place could make or break the career of a singer, a musician, even a television executive. Roddy became arrogant, overbearing, rude, and cruel. Within a year of his having regained his inheritance he had become a superstar.

Although Roddy Abel never hesitated to grant audiences to the faithful, especially when they happened to be members of the press, he never told a soul about the strange man whose last words to him had been a softly murmured, "Ten years, then." Oh, Roddy made great use of the stories of how he had suffered when he was down and out. He had his routine worked out to such a fine degree that he could make his listeners laugh or cry with the slight movement of an eyebrow, or some other such insignificant gesture. And they loved it, every moment of it, because he was one of their favorite heroes and could do no wrong.

When Roddy failed to show up on time at a preholiday season party being given by one of Hollywood's reigning glamour queens, who had flown in from the West Coast especially for the occasion, everyone was disappointed. No one was much worried. From the hostess down to the last guest everybody was certain that Roddy would eventually appear. Not one of them dreamed that Roddy would never be seen alive again, and each became progressively more annoyed as the evening progressed. Concern for his well-being first turned to mild annoyance, and then to anger sparked by viciousness. Of course, none of them had the vaguest notion that Roddy Abel had an appointment to keep, an appointment he had made ten years ago. But Roddy remembered. He remembered well.

The night before, he had gone to sleep very late with a terrible headache. The only thing that had seemed to help it, he found, was to lie down and remain as quiet as possible. After several attempts to get up, only to find that he had a chorus of little men with sledgehammers in his head, he finally cancelled all appointments for the evening and went to bed. Sleep came very quickly, but with sleep came dreams, frightening dreams of falling through space, dreams of being trapped in a burning building, dreams of running along the railroad tracks, a locomotive bearing down on him, and his feet getting heavier, heavier, heavier, till they were like immovable lead weights, as the train came closer, closer, and closer. Then, suddenly, he was in the dark, floating as if in some mysterious place far away from earth. He could move his arms and legs, he could turn, he could feel. But he could neither see nor hear. He began making swimming motions and soon found himself moving along as if he were underwater, though somehow still able to breathe. Something made him move faster, and before long his arms and legs tired. Then, just as suddenly as everything else had happened, he was standing on a hard, pedestallike object. He felt very hot. He tried to open his eyes but they burned too fiercely. He was blinded by something brilliant and painful. It was the sort of feeling he imagined he might experience after staring into the sun through binoculars. Now he was terrified. His heart began pounding. He tried to turn and run, but he could not. It was as if he had turned to stone. Then the voice began calling his name. Softly at first, but gradually becoming louder.

"Who's there?" he tried to cry, but his

vocal cords seemed paralyzed and he couldn't utter a sound.

Then, without any warning, everything changed again. He could open his eyes, he was no longer paralyzed or hot. He began to run. He was in a long narrow corridor with smooth walls, ceiling, and floor. He was afraid he would lose his footing and fall down, but he was able to keep running. The voice continued calling his name, and the more he ran the louder it became. That was when he felt the hand on his arm and he stopped.

Images began going past his eyes like a film running backward. Everything was happening to him, but at the same time he was outside somewhere, watching himself, as if on a giant screen. There he was, shabbily dressed, a stubble of a beard beginning to show on his face, and stopping him on the steps of the public library was an elderly man wearing a dark, nondescript suit.

"Tomorrow will be ten years," he said. "You must be ready for me. Remember our bargain."

That was when Roddy woke up. It was six o'clock in the morning and still quite dark. His forehead was bathed in sweat. The headache was gone, but his heart was still pounding. It was only a dream, he tried to tell himself. It had to be nothing but a dream. Then it dawned on him. The hand on his arm. He could still feel it there. He switched on the lamp alongside his bed and looked at his right arm. There was nothing there. But he could feel a hand holding onto his bicep. He tried to brush it off, but the feeling was still there. Ripping off his pajama top he looked at the arm again. There was an ugly reddish handmark there, in exactly the place that he could still feel the hand gripping him.

He brushed at it again and again, but nothing happened. Nothing would make the mark go away. "I know," he said aloud to himself, looking at his reflection in the mirror. "I'll take a shower. That'll do it." But it didn't. There was only one thing left for him to do, go find the man and plead with him for more time. Ten years seemed like nothing now. Why, he had twenty, thirty, forty years ahead of him.

Hastily he dressed in slacks, an old sweater, and the darkest, least noticeable sport jacket he owned, which he then took off again and replaced with a fleece-lined ski jacket. Dark glasses and a wool pullover cap completed it. He could go out now with every hope of avoiding recognition on the street. Besides, it was still dark. He would go to the library. The man was bound to be there waiting. He knew.

But he was wrong. Just as he got to the front door of his apartment the chimes rang. It never occurred to him that this was a peculiar hour for anyone to come calling. Besides, it was impossible for anyone who did not live in the building to get in without being announced by the night man in the lobby. He opened the door. There, standing in the shadows, smiling slightly, was the elderly man he had met on the steps of the library, looking exactly as he had ten years ago. At the same moment he noticed that he no longer felt the hand on his right arm.

"I expect I'm a little early," said the man softly. "But then, I didn't suppose you had anything more pressing today."

*As a matter of fact, I did!* Roddy wanted to say, but the words stuck in his throat. There were other things he wanted to say, too, like, *Look, mister, why don't you go back where you came from?* or *Why don't we just forget the whole thing?* But none of them came out. All he could manage to croak out in a very weak voice was, "Can't we talk this over?" It was a dumb line that he had heard in just about every grade B movie he ever saw. But it was all he could think of.

"A bargain made is a debt unpaid, Mr. Abel. I have fulfilled my part of it, now it's your turn. Shall we go?"

Roddy tried to back off, but his feet seemed glued to the floor — just like in the dream, when he was on the railroad tracks. But this was no dream and he couldn't move. He glanced at his wristwatch. "It's only six-forty five in the morning . . . I mean . . . can we . . . can't I have just a little more time. The day isn't over until midnight . . . I mean, technically. Right?"

The stranger sighed and folded his arms across his chest. "Mr. Abel," he said, "ten years have passed and eternity lies ahead. Surely, a few miserable hours don't mean that much to you. Come, let's go over to the window — don't be afraid, I won't push you out."

He entered the room, walked past Roddy, and went over to the broad, floor-to-ceiling picture window that looked out over the city from its soaring, thirty-story-high vantage point. As he pulled the drawstring on the drape, the awesome sight of the awakening city spread out before them. Dawn was breaking and the cloak of night was making way for the light of a new day. Far below the streetlights were winking out. The great electric signs had long since gone dark, and the city was just beginning to flex its muscles of steel and concrete in preparation for the assault of another day.

"Look out there, Mr. Abel, and what do you see?" began the man. "Misery and poverty, crime and corruption, pollution and decay. Surely you can't seriously wish to remain as it all rots and deteriorates around you."

*But I don't see all the things you're talking about,* Roddy tried to say. *I know they're there, but I don't see them. I see beauty, I feel excitement, I think of the future!* But the words wouldn't form. "No... No..." was all he could manage to whisper.

"I knew you would finally see things in their proper light," said the man, taking Roddy by the arm and leading him out onto the terrace. "Do you see those dark clouds up

70

there, Mr. Abel?" he continued, pointing up. Roddy looked skyward. "Have you any idea of how much noxious poison they contain? The figures would make you positively ill. Positively ill."

A chill suddenly enveloped Roddy, and he shivered. The clouds seemed to be getting darker and more threatening. It occurred to him that he seemed to be walking through a cloud now, or at least a heavy fog. Strange. He had never seen it so thick on the terrace before. Perhaps if he kept walking it would clear up and then he could find his way back. But then, it was funny, he couldn't quite remember where he was going, or where he had come from. That was when he noticed the elderly man standing alongside him. He felt better. He wasn't alone after all, maybe the gentleman would help him find his way. He seemed to have such a kindly smile.

# THE ESTATE

FROM THE MOMENT they left the six-lane superhighway and began following the twisting, narrow, asphalt back roads, time seemed to go backward. Rambling old houses surrounded by ageless trees looked like remnants of a bygone era. Old-fashioned gas pumps, standing like sentries in front of empty gas stations, made them think of scenes from late-night black and white movies on television. Old cemeteries, overgrown with weeds and tall grass that nearly obscured the weather beaten tombstones, seemed to heighten the depressing atmosphere that clung to the countryside like a moldy old blanket.

This backward, poor, and relatively untouched section of the state was no proper place for a honeymoon, but the young newlyweds were too concerned with reaching their destination to think about anything but the new adventure of starting a new life together. The circumstances were perfect. They had just finished school, gotten married, and between them had about a thousand dollars and a secondhand car. Jobs were scarce, they couldn't afford to go abroad with so little money, and to have taken an apartment in the city would have eaten up their resources before they even had a chance to get started. For those reasons, and others, they had eagerly accepted the offer to stay rent-free at the cottage upstate. In their case, the isolation of the place had made it all the more appealing.

According to what the man told them when they answered the ad in the newspaper, it had originally been a gardener's cottage. It was part of a seven-hundred-acre estate that had been unoccupied for over thirty years. The main house was a fifty-two room mansion that had been built in the early 1800's by an eccentric European man of mystery. He had been very wealthy, a man of refined tastes, but he had lived like a recluse behind walls, fences, and other impassable barriers in a little world of his own making. The stones of the house had been brought over from his native Germany, one at a time. Servants had been imported from several countries, and the estate had been run like a medieval dukedom. Shortly before he died, a nephew from Denmark had come with his wife. They inherited the estate and lived on it until they died many years later. They had had a big family, and in addition to transforming the place into a profitable, self-sustaining farm, had established reputations for themselves as warmhearted, neighborly people, but like their late uncle, closemouthed when it came to revealing anything about themselves or their background.

The descendents of the original builder continued to live on the estate until the late nineteen twenties. After losing their money in the great stock market crash of 1929 the land was abandoned, save for a succession of caretakers. Now, its once elegant mansion crumbling with decay, its formerly lush gardens tangled with weeds, and its fruitful fields barren, the estate was awaiting its final death blow. The bank that owned the property was planning to break up the land into small parcels to be sold off individually. The mansion, the cottages, the barns, and the other outbuildings were to be torn down, and another small piece of the past was to be indecently buried without benefit of a proper funeral.

John and Molly Torney, however, knew nothing of the estate's past. All they were aware of was that they had been given the opportunity to spend an entire summer, rent-free in a charming old cottage. All they had to do in return was to show the land to occasional prospective buyers who might drive up during the time they were there. They would have to rough it a bit. There was no hot water, no telephone, and no electricity. But there were ample old-fashioned kerosene lamps, candles, and a huge open fireplace in the cottage. A stove that operated on bottled gas was the only modern convenience, but that didn't bother them in the least, for they were both young and adventuresome. There were still old fruit trees on the property that would provide them with apples, pears, and cherries. There was a private lake in which to swim, there were wooded lanes to explore, and a vegetable garden that would have been the envy of any amateur farmer.

Before leaving the city they had been instructed by the man from the bank to stop off first in the village, five miles down the road from the main gate of the estate. There they were to see an old man named Henry Adam, who had been the last caretaker for the property, but who was now retired. He would spend a morning out there with them, show them around, and familiarize them with the area in general.

He was a lean old man with a great shock of iron gray hair. "So you're the young folks who'll be staying on the old von Niemand place," he said. He fixed them with piercing pale blue eyes, without smiling, in a way that made Molly feel distinctly uncomfortable. Without any preliminaries, he went with them to their car, climbed into the back seat, and proceeded to give directions.

"Take a left up there about two hundred feet," he ordered, pointing a long gnarled finger.

At that point John couldn't see a thing, but he slowed down and sure enough they soon came to a turnoff at the side of the road. A weatherbeaten sign to the right said *No Trespassing — Private Road*. It was so uninviting, and so easy to miss, John suspected that trespassers were hardly a problem. They followed a bumpy unpaved twisting road that curved through a tangled wood of dense brush, rotted stumps, and pools of stagnant water. Dead trees, lying horizontal among the living ones, and others half dead or dying, stuck out at odd angles.

The retired caretaker, recognizing the look of dismay on Molly's face, inclined his head slightly toward the trees. "Lumber company came up here a few years back. Went through the place like a pack of locusts. Didn't find the kind of timber they were looking for so they left it like this."

"That's terrible," said Molly.

"Better slow down," replied the old man. "Main gate's just up ahead."

"I wonder what he considers fast," thought John to himself, looking at the speedometer. The needle hovered on the slow side of twenty miles per hour. A sharp turn in the road explained the warning. The curve could not have been taken at over 15 M.P.H. Beyond it was a pair of huge marble griffins, one on either side of the road. Perched atop oblong stone pedestals they glared mutely out as if to discourage any strangers who might be tempted to pass through the closed iron gate between them. It was chained and locked with a massive black padlock that looked like a museum piece.

"You two wait here while I unlock it," said the old man.

As he climbed out of the car, Molly inched over to her husband. "I hope it's more cheerful on the inside," she said.

"It's bound to be," answered John. "These old-timers always built their places with gates like this. They kept unfriendly natives out."

"The walls didn't make getting in easy, either," added Molly pointing.

Extending from the griffins on either side were high stone walls with ugly pointed spikes on top at intervals of about every six inches. Each one seemed to point up that the original von Niemand had not been a hospitable man. There was no more time to say anything in private because Henry Adam had finished opening the gate and, having swung it to one side, was motioning John to drive through.

It was a bright, cool, clear day and by the time old Henry had finished giving John and Molly the "fifty-cent tour" as he called it, they were all considerably more comfortable in one another's company. The cottage proved to be everything they had hoped it would be and all it needed was a little airing out. The gas bottles for the stove were full. There were several steel drums of kerosene in the shed out back, and the old-fashioned wooden icebox even had a fresh fifty-pound block of ice inside. It had been put there the day before by none other than Henry himself, along with a supply of staples that he felt would be sufficient to get the young couple started.

"Well," said Henry finally, pulling a large

gold pocket watch out and looking at it, "I expect it's time for me to get back to town. You won't have any trouble finding your way back here."

"What about the front gate?" asked John.

"Best you leave it open, son."

"If you say so."

"By the way," interrupted Molly, "before you go, Mr. Adam, I wonder if you could tell us what's up that path out there. You didn't show us that section, did you?" She pointed out the window to a densely wooded area just back of the cottage beyond the vegetable garden. A footpath going right through the middle was so covered over by a ceiling of tangled vines and branches that it almost resembled a tunnel.

Henry's eyes narrowed and he squared his jaw. "I wouldn't go in there if I was you," he declared, "You might get lost. Besides, there's nothing to see but a mess of trees and rocks."

"But the path looks as though somebody's been using it," observed John.

"Nobody's used it for over fifty years. Now come on, let's get back to town . . . and don't you two go getting lost out there. It could be weeks before anyone'd find you. Hear me?"

The ride back to town was strained, but when they dropped Henry off at his house he insisted that they come in for coffee.

"Do you mind if we save it for another day?" asked Molly. "I want to shop for a few things before we go back."

"Besides," added John, "we'd like to get back before dark."

"That's a good idea," said Henry. "You city folks are always getting lost, specially after dark. When you get back to the von Niemand place just lock up and stay in after sundown. Me and the missus'll come look in on you in a few days. Take care now."

He got out of the car and stood in his doorway watching them as they drove away.

"I wonder what he meant with that business about locking up and staying in after dark?" asked Molly.

John grinned. "Like he said, he probably thinks we're a pair of real dummies who'll get lost the minute we get away from pavement and streetlights . . . and you know something? He's probably right."

They both laughed and started talking about other things until they got to the grocery store. The proprietor was an affable man whose attitude became even friendlier when he found out that they were going to be staying at the von Niemand place all summer.

"Too bad about what they're doin' to that old place," he sighed, shaking his head. "Tearin' down that mansion, bulldozin' the land. It must've been really somethin' in its day. Course, what with taxes 'n' such the way they are now, even rich folks can't afford to live the way they used to." He sighed and shook his head again, a bit more slowly this time. "The only ones I feel sorry for are the dead. Don't seem to be none of the family left t'stop it, so come next spring the wreckin' crews are comin' in to tear everything down — even the graveyard. . . ."

"Graveyard?" murmured Molly.

"That's right, miss. They're just gonna break up the tombstones, plow 'em under, and leave it like that. Unmarked graves. It just don't seem right."

John looked at Molly, then at the grocer. "I don't understand. Mr. Adam didn't tell us anything about a graveyard. We didn't see any tombstones out there."

"It don't surprise me," replied the older man solemnly. "He probably didn't want to scare you. He believes in all that foolishness that's been goin' around about the place all these years. . . ."

"When are you going to learn to keep your big mouth shut, Sam!" thundered a voice from the doorway. The grocer looked up, his jaw dropping open, the two young people looked around, startled. It was old Henry Adam. He was furious.

"I suspicioned you'd be filling these young folks with all your nonsense. . . ."

"Just hold on there, Henry! You're the one that believes in all that hogwash, not me, and don't you forget it!"

With that the two men began shouting and cursing at one another until Molly finally intervened.

"Stop it, you two!" she shouted. "You ought to be ashamed! Why, you're carrying on like a couple of little boys!"

"Mr. Adam," asked John, jumping into the fray, "does all this have anything to do with that path you didn't want to talk about back on the estate?"

The old man glared at the grocer, ran his gnarled fingers through his hair, then turned to John and said, "If you must know it's the way to the graveyard, and if you want some good advice you'll stay away from it night or day. Now that's all I'm going to say. . . . And remember what I said about locking up after sundown." He looked back at the grocer again and added. "I'll talk to you later, Sam."

With that, old Henry Adam walked out of the door without saying another word.

For a moment the three left in the grocery store just stood there, then John turned to the man behind the counter. "Look, Sam," he said, his voice tinged with impatience. "Would you please tell us what this is all about — straight, no double-talk, no commercials?"

"You're not gonna like it."

"I didn't ask you for a bedtime story."

"Y'ain't gonna get one, son. Like I said, I don't believe in all that hogwash about spirits and devils and whatnot. But there is somethin' mighty queer about that place. Maybe no one told you this, but no stranger has ever been able to stay on that property for more than twenty-four hours."

"What happened to them?" demanded Molly.

81

"Can't say for sure. None of 'em ever stuck around long enough to tell."

"Are you suggesting? . . ."

"I ain't suggestin' nothin'. I just don't know. . . . Fact is they just disappeared. If you ask me they got scared an' cleared out."

"Well, what's the story?" asked John, pressing Sam to go on.

"Accordin' to what folks say, old man von Niemand, who built the place, practiced black magic while he was alive. They say that anyone who ever crossed him came to a bad end. That's why no one went near the place but family and hired help while he was alive. Anyway that all changed after he died, except for one thing. Word has it that before he died the old man cast some kind of a spell, like a curse, to protect his property from strangers."

"Well, what was it?" asked Molly impatiently.

"Nobody knows for sure, except that it was supposed to keep out anybody who dared spend more than a single night on the place without family permission."

"And if they did?"

"Somethin' terrible was supposed to happen to 'em."

"Like what?"

"I can't say."

"That's ridiculous," scoffed John.

"That's just what I've been tryin' to tell you two all along!" declared Sam, slapping the counter with the flat of his hand. But then a strange look came into his eye. He cleared his throat. "All the same though," he added, "I'd do like Henry says, and keep the place locked after dark."

The drive back out to the von Niemand place seemed to take forever, and in light of what they had heard in town neither John nor Molly seemed inclined to talk. One thing was certain, each of them knew it without having to say a word aloud. They would not do a thing until they had explored the forbidden path leading to the old family burying ground. Old Henry Adam's attempt to keep them from knowing about it had certainly aroused their curiosity at the outset. But the grocer's tale had served as an out and out challenge.

It was late afternoon when they arrived at the cottage. The sun was turning the sky to a rich wall of gold and the lengthening shadows stretched out across the ground on all sides. Although the air was quite still, the temperature had dropped considerably and Molly insisted that they wear sweaters before they ventured out to investigate the old graveyard.

The overgrowth enveloping the path was so thick that one got the distinct feeling of going through a tunnel. It was somewhat cooler because of the absence of direct light. There was also another absence. Sound. Not a bird, not an insect, not a breeze. Only the crackle of their footsteps on fallen leaves and the crunch of gravel broke the stillness. The heaviness of the silence seemed to discourage talk as they strode through the brush, now clutching one another tightly by the hand.

It was not until they reached the clearing that they realized what a distance they had come, easily a half mile. "Tiny, isn't it," whispered Molly.

"It sure is," replied John.

There before them, surrounded by a black wrought-iron fence that was pitted with rust, was the von Niemand family cemetery. Not more than two dozen tombstones marked the final resting places of those who slumbered beneath the ground. The oldest of them, weatherbeaten with age, were canted at slight angles, and the most recent stood solid and erect.

"Thaddeus von Niemand," read John aloud from the marker nearest them. "Eighteen seventy-one, eighteen ninety-six, foully slain in the springtime of his life by one he thought a friend."

"Creepy, isn't it," observed Molly, shivering slightly.

"I'll bet that's where the old man is buried," said John, pointing to the farthest point at the center of the graveyard. There, dominating the scene, was a gray stone mausoleum carved to resemble a tent. The door resembled a barred prison, and if it had a lock it was not visible. Most impressive, however, were its two granite guardians. Two carved griffins, identical to those that flanked the main gate except for one feature: These griffins clutched upraised swords in their fists.

"Mol, it's still light enough. Let's go in and see if we can get a look at the old boy's coffin."

Instead of answering, she seized John's arm. "Listen," she said. "Did you hear that?"

"What?"

"It was like a groan, way off in the distance."

He grinned. "Oh, come on now, you must be. . . ."

"There, you heard it this time, didn't you?"

A chill came over him. There was no denying it. He did hear it. But there was something else, too. "Did . . . did you hear something like a scraping sound?"

She tried to tell him that she had, but she couldn't find her voice. All she could do was look up and nod. The next thing they knew they were running hand in hand, as fast as they could, back through the thicket toward the house.

They needed no urging that night to do exactly what Henry Adam had warned them to do, stay in and keep everything locked. Frightened as they had been, sleep came easily, for the half-mile sprint from the cemetery to the cottage had taken its toll. They slept so soundly that they never heard a sound, even as the wall of the bedroom seemed to disintegrate before the relentless onslaught of the hideous things that could not exist, but that now loomed up toward the sleepers, their great shaggy wings outstretched, their hideous beaks gaping wickedly open, their granite swords poised on high . . . .

*As he stepped outside the grocery store a subtle change came over Henry Adam's face. The stern expression of anger turned into a look of sly satisfaction. The soft and kindly lines vanished, replaced by hard and cruel contours that might have been chiseled out of granite. His mouth stretched into a tight, thin grin of incredible evil and, as he glanced at the lengthening shadows in the direction of the setting sun, his not quite human eyes glittered with awful anticipation. . . .*

# THE EVIL EYE

I WAS VERY YOUNG then, poor as a church mouse, and half the time cold and hungry to boot. But somehow, I managed to live. I had found a place to stay in the garret of an ancient house on a twisting, narrow, garbage-strewn street off the Rue Madelaine. I felt sometimes like a bird that had made its nest in a roof, for I slept on a straw mattress in the middle of the room, over which I had to climb in order to get to the window. But the climb was worth it, for through the window's dingy panes I could see the streets of Paris below. I could see processions of gaunt cats walking precariously along gutters, pigeons and starlings going about their daily business, and, at night beady-eyed rats foraging for scraps of booty.

Every evening when the church bells summoned the faithful to their prayers, I would rest my arms on the sill and listen to the ringing near and far. I would watch the windows light up one at a time; the Parisians hurrying through the streets with loaves of bread and bottles of wine under their arms. I tried to memorize the faces of the laughing young girls and the sour old men. Then, when darkness fell I could hear the flapping of wings as bats began to gather, and I knew it was once again time for other things.

There was an elderly second-hand dealer named Trevec who used to visit me weekly. He knew the way to my little aerie as well as I did, and whenever I heard the scraping of feet on the rusty ladder, I knew that it was the old man. Each time he came, his head would pop up through the creaky trap door, and as he grabbed the floor for support, he would cry out, "Bon soir, Monsieur Jean Paul, have you anything to sell today?"

To which I would reply, "Come in, my friend, don't just stand there. I'm just putting the finishing touches on a new oil. Come see, and tell me what you think of it."

Then he would pull himself up into my garret, cautiously straighten out lest he crack his head on the roof, and peer at my latest work. He would look first from one side, and then from the other. Next he would stroke his whiskers thoughtfully, grunt a few times, and offer me ten francs. It was a little game we played. No matter what I painted he always paid me ten francs. No more, no less. We never bargained, and we both knew he would take my masterpieces to his little shop and sell them for twenty-five. The arrangement suited both of us, and in time I came to be very happy, in spite of my poverty.

Not too far from my little window, diagonally off to the left, was the old Hotel Chez Moucheron. It was an unpretentious little place and was patronized mostly by foreigners and countrymen from the provinces. The gables of its roof came to narrow sharp points that resembled the inverted teeth of some monstrous beast of great dimension. The windows were intricately carved with grotesque shapes that also carried through on all the cornices and gutters. What intrigued me, however, was the fact that directly across from the hotel was a house that might have been its mirror image. Every detail present in the hotel was there in the house, but in reverse. The two buildings were hundreds of years old, and must have been put up by a single builder. And although they reflected each other in appearance, they were different from each other in another respect. Whereas the hotel was always bustling with guests, an endless procession of humanity, laughing, talking, cursing, and otherwise carrying on, the house across the way was quiet as a tomb.

It was not deserted though, for once or twice each day the massive front door of the place would open slowly, and out would come a bent old hag who was ugly beyond belief. Her chin was pointed, and from it sprouted scraggly wisps of gray hair. Though the hair on her head was as gray as that on her chin, her eyebrows were bushy and black, and her dress was even blacker. Whenever she went out she clutched a huge basket under one arm while the other was clutched against her chest as if she expected her wrapper to blow open at any moment.

I took to watching her closely whenever I

could, for her face was as fascinating as it was hideous. Her eyes were beady and green, like stagnant water. Her nose was like the beak of a bird of prey, and her wrinkled cheeks reminded me of leather. Most of the time she was wrapped in an antique-looking shawl that appeared to be at least twice her age, and the old lace cap on her head reminded me of pictures I had seen in the Louvre depicting women of centuries past. There was something so strange about her that my curiosity was aroused and I was determined to learn who this old woman might be, and what it was that she did all alone in her dark and silent house.

For a time I pictured her as a pious old soul who devoted her life to contemplation and charitable works. But then, one day as I was returning from the market, I met her in the street and stopped to stare at her. She passed me as though I were not there, but suddenly she stopped, turned around, and gave me a glare of such horrible malice that even today I am at a loss to describe its sheer ugliness. The moment that her eyes met mine a chill went down my spine, and though I wanted to turn and flee, I could not. I was helplessly caught by her withering grimace. Happily for me, she finally drew her shawl about her, turned around, and went directly to her house, finally disappearing behind the massive front door.

"She must be mad," I thought to myself. And to think, I had imagined her a kindly old soul. But then I smiled. My interest in her had not been a waste of time. Trevec would gladly pay me ten francs for her hideous expression properly preserved on canvas.

Unfortunately, the matter did not end quite so abruptly as all that. At first I thought it was simply a matter of my not being able to get the old harpy's face out of my mind. But then, whenever I encountered her, and regardless of the circumstances, she always regarded me with that terrible grimace. Not only that, on more than one occasion while I was climbing the ladder to my garret I imagined I could feel my clothes being seized from behind by something, someone. And in my nightmares I came to understand that it was the old woman.

After some time I told the whole story to Trevec, half expecting him to ridicule me for a fool. On the contrary, he listened to me in all solemnity, and when I had finished he said to me, "Monsieur Jean Paul, you must beware. If the old crone means you any harm at all, you may be in danger. Have you seen her teeth?"

I nodded,

"*Alors!*" he declared. "Then you have observed they are tiny and pointed and sparkling white ... a very unnatural thing for a woman of her age. It is said she possesses the Evil Eye, and I for one believe this to be true. Children flee at her approach, and for good reason. She is known to the people of the district as 'The Bat.' "

What Trevec had said gave me good cause

to think, but after several weeks of seeing The Bat frequently, without suffering anything more painful than the sting of her glance, I became less nervous, and concluded that whether the old woman made faces at me or not, if I were careful climbing my ladder I would avoid catching my clothes on protruding nails in the wall, and then I would not have to look over my shoulder in the dark. So in time I came to pay no more attention to The Bat when we met.

Some time later, two or three months perhaps, I was awakened from a sound sleep in the middle of the night. There were no sounds in the streets, but still I had heard something. I knew it was in my garret. It was hard to describe — a soft vibration, a fluttering. It was so unfamiliar that I became alarmed. Then I thought that maybe my mind was playing tricks on me. But suddenly, as my gaze reached the window, I caught sight of something that made the blood freeze in my veins. There, shimmering hideously, the light of the moon filtering through it, was a grinning skull. I hoped and prayed that I was only dreaming, that I was in the grip of some terrible nightmare. But it was no use, I was awake and I knew it. Then as my eyes grew accustomed to the gloom, I became aware that it was no apparition I beheld, but a living creature even more helpless than myself — a giant death's-head moth. Somehow it had gotten trapped in my chamber. Sighing with relief, I arose from my pallet, opened the skylight, and turned the insect loose into the night.

It was clear and warm, I recall. In the heavens above thousands of glittering stars clustered like diamonds about a brilliant full moon. For a few moments I stood there, drinking in the beauty before me, when my reverie was interrupted by still another strange sound, this time outside. Leaning over the edge of the window I peered out, and immediately gasped. Imagine my horror when I saw, swinging gently to and fro from the stanchion supporting the sign of the Hotel Moucheron, the body of a man. The sound I had heard, God help me, was the creaking of the rope against the stanchion. He was quite dead. His jaw hung slack, his eyes bulged open, staring sightless upon the deserted street, his arms and legs dangled limply down.

It was a dreadful sight. For a moment I remained motionless, staring in morbid fascination. Then a chill overcame me. My teeth began chattering, and for a reason I cannot explain, I turned away and fixed my glance on the window of the mirror-image house across the way. To my amazement I saw the old woman, crouched in the dark, peering out at the hanging body. A hiddeous grin exposed her gleaming white teeth. Spittle ran down the side of her mouth, and she rocked back and forth rubbing her gnarled hands together in a gesture of malevolent relish. The diabolical gleam in her glittering green eyes was so dreadful that I could no longer restrain myself. I might have uttered an outcry of dismay but, before the sound could rise from my throat, I leaped up and at the same time cracked my head on the roof beam, thus losing consciousness before I collapsed to the floor.

I must have lain there all night, for when I regained my senses the light of day flooded into the garret. My head throbbed with the pain of a hundred hammers, but the sound of tumult and excitement from the street below forced me to drag myself up so that I might look down and see what it was.

There, gathered around the entrance of the Hotel Moucheron was an excited crowd of citizens and children, gesturing, shouting, and chattering all at once as the gendarmes directed two carriers bearing a shrouded stretcher away. The crowd followed, an informal funeral procession, and soon they were gone. Once more I directed my glance to the stanchion holding the signboard of the hotel. There, freshly cut, was the remaining piece of rope. I now knew that I had not dreamed a thing: the death's head moth, the hanging man, and the cackling old hag in her dismal old house.

Later that day my friend Trevec came to call. "Have you anything new for me this week, Monsieur Jean Paul?" he cried.

So absorbed in thought was I that I scarcely heard him.

"Monsieur Jean Paul," he repeated, placing

his hand on my shoulder and shaking me gently. "What's wrong?"

"Oh, Trevec!" I exclaimed looking up.

"The same. Tell me, are you unwell?"

"No. I was just thinking, that's all."

"About what, may I ask?"

"About the man who was hanged."

"*Alors!* You saw him, eh?"

I nodded wordlessly.

Trevec shook his head and sighed. "Very strange. Very strange indeed! It's the third hanging in the very same place."

"The third hanging?"

"*Oui, mon ami,* and I fear there will be a fourth and a fifth ... and who knows how many more?"

"Tell me about the other two." I insisted.

Trevec sat down, stroking his whiskers thoughtfully, and began to talk. "I'm not a fearful man myself, Monsieur, but I'd as soon spend the night up to my chin in a barrel of rainwater as sleep in that room. Nine or ten months ago an Englishman from London came to the Moucheron. He ate his dinner in the public room, seemed cheerful — even spoke proper French — then, when he was done, the serving girl showed him to his room. It was the one on the third floor that they call 'the yellow chamber. . . .' " Here Trevec paused, leaned forward, and lowered his voice. "The next morning they found his body swinging from the stanchion. Well, there was quite a hubbub, you can be sure. The gendarmes came, and Monsieur Gaudin, the hotelier was disconsolate. A hearing was held and of course poor M. Gaudin was not held responsible; after a few weeks had passed the affair was forgotten. But then, about two months later, a peasant from the provinces came along. He was a big, gruff, jovial fellow, who laughed and told coarse stories the moment he set foot in the hotel. All evening long he drank wine and entertained the company until at last it was bedtime. He, too, was shown to the yellow chamber. And the next morning, *voila!* they found him hanging from the stanchion.

"Now, you can imagine what a scandal it was this time. Two in a row. The neighborhood was up in arms. It was suggested to M. Gaudin that he take down his stanchion, and that if he didn't do it himself, he might be forced to do so. Of course he wouldn't hear of it. 'No!' he said. 'My great grandfather put up that stanchion, and by heaven it stays there! The stanchion hasn't killed anyone! Those poor sinners did it themselves in violation of the laws of God and man!'

"So, the stanchion remained and, tempers finally cooling off, the neighborhood settled down to normal again. Nothing out of the way happened until last night."

"There has to be more to it than that!" I cried, clenching my fists, and beating the air. "Does no one wish to bring this dreadful parade of deaths to a halt? Surely there is some dark and terrible secret behind them, and I suspect that neither the chamber nor the stanchion is at the bottom of the mystery!"

"Monsieur Jean Paul!" exclaimed Trevec. Certainly you do not suggest that perhaps M. Gaudin is responsible! *Sacre bleu!* He is the model of virtue, a pillar of the community...."

"I make no accusations, Trevec, I assure you. I merely say that there are forces of evil in this world so unspeakable that we hardly dare think of them. Yet they exist!"

"Perhaps they do, Monsieur," agreed Trevec reluctantly, then crossing himself as an afterthought. "And for that very reason, I suggest that we do not speak of the unspeakable. Tell me, how is work progressing on your painting of the Place de la Concorde?"

His question served to bring both of us back to the everyday world of reality. After showing the dealer the painting about which he had asked, we concluded our business and shook hands. Then, just before taking his leave of me, Trevec raised his right hand and shook a warning finger at me. "If I were you, Monsieur Jean Paul, I would think no more of this unpleasant business about the yellow chamber." With that he bade me adieu and made his way back down the ladder.

I suppose I should have listened to the old man, but something within gnawed at me, driving me to dwell upon the matter until it became an obsession. I could not purge my mind of the sinister events connected with the yellow chamber and the hag in her house across the way. The memory of her rocking back and forth in the gloom that night, cackling to herself with diabolical glee as the dead man dangled from the stanchion, haunted my every sleeping and waking hour.

The more I thought about it the more convinced I became that she was no ordinary mortal and that she was solely reponsible for the deaths of those innocent men. Perhaps, I thought, she had once been as the rest of us, but was now an instrument of the devil himself. If this was so, I reasoned, what other works of evil might she be brewing in the dark midnight hours while honest folk slept? Could it be that a provident divine force had permitted me to witness her wickedness for some purpose? Could it be that I had been appointed as the instrument of her undoing? For many nights I lay tossing, sleepless and troubled, for such thoughts I recognized to be akin to those of madmen and scoundrels, who twisted events to their own nefarious purposes.

But then, what reason should I have to hate or fear The Bat? She had never done me any harm personally. Certainly I was strong enough to withstand the assault of her grimaces. But three men had died mysteriously. It was no figment of my imagination that I had seen her in the shadows that night. There was only one course of action open to me. I had to observe her until I was absolutely certain of the truth. Unless I accomplished this, I would be undone.

On the night that I came to this decision I arose from my straw, wrapped myself in a black cloak, and hid in the street within sight of her door. It was a lonely vigil, and I encountered none but hungry cats, beady-eyed rats, and other less savory denizens of dark places.

I was rewarded shortly after daybreak, when her door slowly opened and The Bat emerged with her customary basket, her antique shawl trailing behind her. With pounding heart I followed her. Not once did I permit her to leave my sight. Had I been a leech from the great stone crock of the apothecary I could not have kept closer watch over her. She went about her business paying no attention to me, but inwardly I knew she sensed my presence. After many weeks of this kind of fruitless pursuit I felt that I had accomplished nothing. I was especially chilled one evening when her eyes met mine for a brief instant before she disappeared into the gloomy recesses of her house. There was no mistaking the expression: It was one of satisfaction, cunning satisfaction.

As I huddled in the corner of my garret one day reflecting on the events of the weeks past, a chill overcame me. Suppose she had cast some fatal spell over me and snared me in her web of evil. Was the wretched old crone anticipating ere long the sight of my limp form dangling at the end of a rope? If so, I had to foil her and I began cudgeling my brain to arrive at a proper scheme. Then an idea smote me with the unexpectedness of a lightning bolt.

My garret overlooked the house of The Bat, but the side from which one might have had the best view had no window. I quickly

99

solved the problem by stealthily raising one of the shingles of the roof, thus fashioning for myself a perfect peephole through which to observe my quarry and yet remain completely invisible to her.

"Now I shall discover your evil secret," I muttered to myself. "Then we shall see what happens."

The hidden portion of the old woman's abode was exactly what I might have imagined it to be. A dank and filthy yard, enclosed on all sides by a high wall, adjoined the rear of the house. Cracked paving stones, overgrown with moss, filled the entire area. In the far corner stood a well, filled with green and stagnant water, giving rise to the thought that at any moment slimy creatures would creep from it and slither off in the shadows. As for the house itself, a rickety staircase led to a cluttered rear balcony guarded by a balustrade with a number of broken rails. From it hung a stained and dirty mattress tick that looked to be infested with lice.

The back wall of the house was of damp gray stone, covered with irregular splotches of ugly mold. The entire area was so enclosed that even when the sun was at its zenith it was shrouded in gloomy shadows. It seemed a proper setting for its malignant proprietress. I was confident that I would soon achieve my purpose.

On the day that I first devised my scheme of spying upon The Bat from a secret hiding place it was late afternoon. I determined to wait until the following day to begin my vigil. Darkness came late, for it was midsummer and the heat was so oppressive that sleep came only in fitful moments of short duration.

After an early, hasty breakfast at a tiny cafe on the Rue Madelaine, I hurried back to my chamber to begin my vigil. Enclosed as I was in the tiny garret, I felt as I imagined a bird would feel roasting in an oven, but despite my discomfort I remained at my vantage point.

I had barely stood watch for three-quarters of an hour when I saw the old harpy emerge from the door of her kitchen on the second floor. With a gait more spritely than one might imagine one of her age able to employ, and carrying a rough, homemade broom that added to her witchlike appearance, she descended the stairs to the yard. After half-heartedly sweeping the paving stones, she crossed back to the stairs where she suddenly stopped in her tracks. Raising her head, she looked directly at the roof behind which I was hidden. As she scanned it with her piercing green eyes, I shuddered, despite the scorching heat, for it was as though her stare had succeeded in penetrating the shingles, enabling her to look directly at me. It might well have been my imagination. At any rate, she finally averted her eyes and returned to the house as if nothing out of the ordinary had happened. I could not be sure, but I was so unnerved by her look, I decided to devote the rest of the day to beginning a new painting. I was down to my last few sous, and if I did not have something for Trevec when he paid me my weekly visit, I would not only risk going hungry, but would incur the wrath of my landlord as well.

I resumed my watch early the next morning. When The Bat made her appearance she seemed to be in a jovial mood. Although I could not hear her, she seemed to be humming to herself. She went down to the yard, busied herself there for a while, and then, displaying that incredible agility I had observed in her, began chasing a large horsefly, which she presently caught with her bare hands. Holding it by one wing, she held it up before her face and cackled as it struggled and buzzed to get free. Then, returning to the stairs, she climbed to the top and went directly to the far corner of the balcony. I raised the shingle ever so slightly higher so that I could see what she was up to, and just in time too. Raising one hand, the one that held the fly, she appeared at first to be waving it before the overhanging roof above, a mad gesture, I thought. But then I discovered her purpose. There, dangling from a gossamer thread below a gray and tangled web was an immense black spider. She was feeding the ugly thing the same way honest folk fed tidbits to decent animals. There was something about her manner that made me shudder.

As the days passed, I came to comprehend

that the crone had no companion save the spider, which she frequently fawned over like a well-loved pet. Nothing else out of the ordinary occurred. Nevertheless, I continued spying upon her.

After a while I began to lose heart. Trevec complained that the quality of my work was declining, and that if I did not improve it he would, reluctantly, take his business elsewhere. I promised him that I would do as he said, and he patted me on the shoulder and assured me that he would see me the following week. Then he left me alone.

Darkness was descending, and I looked through my window. Had I fallen victim to a foolish obsession? Was I merely playing the fool, squandering my time prying into the private affairs of a harmless, if unpleasant, old woman? More out of habit than anything else, I went to the loose shingle, moved it up, and peered through my eyehole. Just then The Bat emerged from her kitchen door, looking as I had never seen her look before. Her stride was determined, her neck muscles stood out, her jaw was firmed with an expression of strange resolution. Her long gray hair hung loose as she bent over a heap of rags and rummaged about before going back inside the house. I was certain that there had been a gleam of anticipation in her eyes, an evil, vicious look that filled me with apprehension. Something was afoot. I knew it.

Determined to keep the watch this one last night, I stretched out upon my pallet with my hands folded behind my head to rest for a while and wait until it was completely dark. As I lay there, casually wondering what had made her behave so strangely, I glanced up at my skylight window and noticed a light that had not been there the previous evening. I jumped up and looked out. To my horror I could see clearly that the yellow chamber had a light in it. Heaven help the stranger, whoever he might be, for his life was in mortal danger. I had to do something, but what?

Peering through my peephole I strained to see what the old harridan was up to and, sure enough, I could see her in the gloom, peering through her window, watching every movement of the occupant of the yellow chamber. As my eyes grew accustomed to the darkness I could see her face clearly. The expression she wore reminded me of that of an undertaker, measuring a corpse for its coffin.

After several hours, the light in the yellow chamber went out and The Bat disappeared from her hiding place. I knew that the stranger was safe for this night, so I abandoned my watch and went to bed, falling soon into a fitful sleep.

The next morning I was awake at dawn. I had barely gotten to my lookout when I saw The Bat emerge from her kitchen door clad in a gray flannel wrapper. Her eyes were red, her hair dishevelled. Suddenly, she dashed down the stairs to her yard like one pursued. Then, after checking the wall on all four sides, for what reason I know not, she ran back to the stairs and bounded up them with the speed and agility of a maid in her twenties. This time, instead of going into the kitchen, she stopped before another door that I had never seen her open. Thrusting a large, rusty key into the lock, she fumbled for a moment, then pushed the door open. Its ancient hinges creaked as if in protest and she slipped inside, closing it again behind her. Though I could not see, I strained to listen for any telltale sounds that might provide me with a hint of what she was doing behind the creaky door. For a moment there was silence, then came the unmistakable scraping noise of something very heavy being dragged across a floor. Again, all was silent. At last I heard a muted slam like the falling of a heavy lid on a chest — or a coffin. The creaking of the door announced the old woman's reappearance, and I concentrated to see — a difficult feat in the gathering darkness. Instead of coming out in the normal fashion, she backed out. At first I could hardly believe my eyes, for as she stopped to close the door I could have sworn that she was dragging a dead body behind her. My heart leaped! But then I saw what it was — no man born of woman, dead or alive, but a life-sized mannequin dressed in the identical attire of the last poor wretch to die at the end of a rope dangling from the stanchion of the Hotel Moucheron!

It was what she did next that really inspired my shudders. After stretching the mannequin out to its full length she fastened a rope with a hangman's knot around its neck. Cackling with devilish glee, she tightened it, threw the opposite end over a roof beam, and strung the figure up with the dexterous and practiced hand of a seasoned hangman. For a moment or so she stood back, hugging herself and rocking to and fro in rhythm with the swaying mannequin, filling the air with terrible peals of laughter. Suddenly she stopped dead and cocked her head to listen. A noise from the street distracted her. She darted into the kitchen, returned with a lighted lantern a few moments later, and bolted down the stairs to her yard below. Raising the lantern above her head she contemplated the dangling figure above for a moment, then bounded back up the stairs with the speed and energy of a spritely girl, put the lantern down, and sprang at the hanging figure, which she proceeded to take down from its beam. Then, without hesitation, she dragged it back to the mysterious chamber with the creaky door and disappeared briefly inside. Again I could hear the familiar lid slamming down. Seconds later she reappeared at the door, making certain to lock it. After that she picked up her lantern and retreated back into the gloomy recesses of her house.

Although I was unable to understand the exact meaning of all her activities, I feared the worst.

Early the next morning I resumed my watch once again. At nine o'clock on the stroke, The Bat emerged from the house, the familiar basket under one arm, and the long shawl trailing behind her. Gone were the signs of agility, and once again she moved with the tottering gait of an aged old crone. I watched her until she passed beyond my line of view. Busying myself for the next five hours, I frequently peered through my eyehole, awaiting her return. The rising heat turned my poor garret into a furnace, yet I dared not leave. At one point I observed through the skylight that the occupant of the yellow chamber was dressed and ready to take his leave. He wore the uniform of a regiment that had served with the Emperor in the disastrous Russian campaign, and I thought to myself, "Take care, soldier!" What a cruel blow to fate it would be to survive the terrible march home from Moscow, only to perish because of the wicked machinations of a vile witch.

When The Bat finally came home I heard her at the front door. Rushing to my secret lookout I waited till she appeared in the private recesses of the rear balcony above her yard. She was carrying her basket and it was covered with a cloth. Taking it downstairs, she placed it on the ground and, after removing the cloth, proceeded to take out several bunches of vegetables and herbs and a brown paper bundle. When she had finished untying the string she took out the contents, and when I saw what it was I drew back in dismay — a soldier's uniform, identical to the one worn by the man in the yellow chamber!

I now knew her secret. By employing elemental powers available to any who choose to decipher the riddle of their existence, she was able to spin an invisible web of despair about her victims, thereby destroying them. I determined at that moment to turn her own weapons against her.

For the rest of the day I scurried about Monmartre calling upon every second-hand clothes dealer and ragman I could find. By nightfall I returned, but instead of climbing up to my garret, I went directly to the Hotel Moucheron and sought out Monsieur Gaudin.

"*Bon soir*, Monsieur," he said. "What brings you here so unexpectedly?"

"Monsieur Gaudin," I said as earnestly as I could, "I wish very much to spend a night in your mysterious yellow chamber. . . ."

A look of alarm came over his features. He was about to object, but I would not let him interrupt. Wagging a finger of my right hand back and forth, I continued. "Do not be afraid, Monsieur. I have no intention of hanging myself, but I must stay there in connection with a very special painting I am preparing." He sighed with relief.

"I am glad to hear that, Monsieur, for painters with your gifts should be granted long lives. I hope you do not wish to stay there tonight, though. It is occupied. . . ."

"It is no longer!" came a loud and angry voice from behind us. It was the soldier. His face was livid with a mixture of anger and terror. "I have heard the truth about that chamber of horrors! You deserve the guillotine for daring to place innocent men in it! Be thankful, Monsieur, that I choose not to report you to the authorities! If you know what's good for you, you'll seal the accursed room off once and for all. *Adieu!*" With that he threw his bundle over his shoulder and stalked angrily out the door.

Monsieur Gaudin was terribly upset, but I assured him that all was well, and I insisted on being shown to the yellow chamber. Outwardly, it was like all the other rooms in the hotel, simple and unprepossessing. Its only outstanding feature was an immense oak four-poster bed, covered with homemade quilting. From the window there was a direct view of The Bat's house, and, of course, directly below the window extended the stanchion from which the hotel's sign hung.

I looked out. There was not a single light visible across the way. Good, I thought, I shall now have ample time to prepare my little surprise for her.

Closing the curtains, I undid the parcel I had prepared. Removing the contents I set to work and after an hour or so I had finished fashioning a dummy, which in the dark looked reasonably like the old woman's intended victim. But that only completed half my preparations. I next spread out the old gown, cap, and shawl which I proceeded to put on over my own clothes. Then, bending over the looking glass, I took a stick of charcoal and began drawing lines upon my face. I worked slowly and carefully, and having finished, I so resembled the old woman, the illusion was uncanny.

Now I was ready. Placing my dummy in the shadows, in a posture like that of a man in the throes of despair, I lit the candle and

109

placed it in a position where it would provide only enough light to serve my purpose. Cautiously I peered through the curtains. As I had suspected, The Bat was crouched in the shadows behind her own window, scrutinizing the yellow chamber the way a cat does a mouse. Making certain to remain out of sight, I drew back the curtains and brought the dummy forward so that from the outside it would appear to be rising from its place and moving of its own volition.

Stealthily I reached over and opened the casement, observing that across the way The Bat was doing the same thing. In the gloom all she could possibly see was what she believed to be her living prey, kneeling, perhaps weeping, and resting his head against the windowsill. Then the instant she leaned out, I seized my candle, and leaned out myself. The witch and I were now face to face. So shocked was she that her hands flew up, causing her to drop the mannequin clutched between them. She raised a hand to her face. I did the same. She clasped her bosom with the other. I mimicked her. Her eyes widened, so did mine. Not a sound escaped either of our lips, but the tension mounted in a frightful mood of terror. It was unreal! It was uncanny! It was a struggle between two spirits, each trying to overcome the other. After having continued in this fashion for some moments, I reached beneath the gown I wore, drew forth a thick rope, and tied one end to the stanchion. The old woman's expression gradually became one of wide-eyed horror. I grimaced and tied the other end of the rope about my own neck. Her eyeballs fluttered wildly. Her features contorted with disbelief.

"No!" she shrieked. "No!"

I continued securing the rope, as if she were invisible.

"Mercy!" she croaked. "Have mercy on me!"

Then I blew out my candle and bent down like one preparing to leap. With my right hand I seized the dummy beside me, transferred the rope from my neck to its, and hurled it through the window.

A single, strangled shriek shattered the stillness of the night, then trailed off in a whimpering gurgle. Once again silence returned and I heaved a sigh of relief. Across the narrow street, The Bat now dangled lifelessly at the end of a rope suspended from the stanchion beneath her window. As I stood there trembling slightly, the church bells of Paris began pealing the hour of midnight. I closed the curtains and retreated to the yellow chamber.

The next day all of Montmartre was whispering in hushed tones that the district was finally free of the witch, for she had hung herself the night before. And as for the yellow chamber, it was given a fresh coat of blue paint, and was never again known as an evil place to any of its occupants.

*point* ®  **THRILLERS**

### R.L. Stine

☐ MC44236-8 The Baby-sitter $3.25
☐ MC44332-1 The Baby-sitter II $3.25
☐ MC45386-6 Beach House $3.25
☐ MC43278-8 Beach Party $3.25
☐ MC43125-0 Blind Date $3.25
☐ MC43279-6 The Boyfriend $3.25
☐ MC44333-X The Girlfriend $3.25
☐ MC45385-8 Hit and Run $3.25
☐ MC43280-X The Snowman $3.25
☐ MC43139-0 Twisted $3.25

### Caroline B. Cooney

☐ MC44316-X The Cheerleader $3.25
☐ MC41641-3 The Fire $3.25
☐ MC43806-9 The Fog $3.25
☐ MC45681-4 Freeze Tag (11/92) $3.25
☐ MC45402-1 The Perfume $3.25
☐ MC44884-6 Return of the Vampire $2.95
☐ MC41640-5 The Snow $3.25

### Diane Hoh

☐ MC44330-5 The Accident $3.25
☐ MC45401-3 The Fever $3.25
☐ MC43050-5 Funhouse $3.25
☐ MC44904-4 The Invitation $2.95
☐ MC45640-7 The Train (9/92) $3.25

### Sinclair Smith

☐ MC45063-8 The Waitress $2.95

### Christopher Pike

☐ MC43014-9 Slumber Party $3.25
☐ MC44256-2 Weekend $3.25

### A. Bates

☐ MC45829-9 The Dead Game (12/92) $3.25
☐ MC43291-5 Final Exam $3.25
☐ MC44582-0 Mother's Helper $2.95
☐ MC44238-4 Party Line $3.25

### D.E. Athkins

☐ MC45246-0 Mirror, Mirror $3.25
☐ MC45349-1 The Ripper (10/92) $3.25
☐ MC44941-9 Sister Dearest $2.95

### Carol Ellis

☐ MC44768-8 My Secret Admirer $3.25
☐ MC44916-8 The Window $2.95

### Richie Tankersley Cusick

☐ MC43115-3 April Fools $3.25
☐ MC43203-6 The Lifeguard $3.25
☐ MC43114-5 Teacher's Pet $3.25
☐ MC44235-X Trick or Treat $3.25

### Lael Littke

☐ MC44237-6 Prom Dress $3.25

### Edited by T. Pines

☐ MC45256-8 Thirteen $3.50

Available wherever you buy books, or use this order form.

**Scholastic Inc., P.O. Box 7502, 2931 East McCarty Street, Jefferson City, MO 65102**

Please send me the books I have checked above. I am enclosing $_____ (please add $2.00 to cover shipping and handling). Send check or money order — no cash or C.O.D.s please.

Name _____

Address_____

City_____ State/Zip_____
Please allow four to six weeks for delivery. Offer good in the U.S. only. Sorry, mail orders are not available to residents of Canada. Prices subject to change.                PT192